C0-ABK-552

SPECIAL MESSAGE TO READERS

THE ULVERSCROFT FOUNDATION
(registered UK charity number 264873)
was established in 1972 to provide funds for research, diagnosis and treatment of eye diseases.
Examples of major projects funded by the Ulverscroft Foundation are:-

- The Children's Eye Unit at Moorfields Eye Hospital, London
- The Ulverscroft Children's Eye Unit at Great Ormond Street Hospital for Sick Children
- Funding research into eye diseases and treatment at the Department of Ophthalmology, University of Leicester
- The Ulverscroft Vision Research Group, Institute of Child Health
- Twin operating theatres at the Western Ophthalmic Hospital, London
- The Chair of Ophthalmology at the Royal Australian College of Ophthalmologists

You can help further the work of the Foundation by making a donation or leaving a legacy. Every contribution is gratefully received. If you would like to help support the Foundation or require further information, please contact:

THE ULVERSCROFT FOUNDATION
The Green, Bradgate Road, Anstey
Leicester LE7 7FU, England
Tel: (0116) 236 4325

website: www.ulverscroft-foundation.org.uk

LOVE AND LIES

When Rosie Peach arrives for her interview to become Shaston Convent School's new piano teacher, the first person she meets is striking music master David Hart. As her new role gets underway, Rosie comes up against several obstacles: her predecessor Miss Spiker's infamous temper, a bunch of unruly but loveable schoolgirls, and her swiftly growing feelings for David. The nuns of the convent are determined to meddle their way towards a school romance, but David is a complex character, and Rosie can't help but wonder what secrets he is hiding . . .

JENNY WORSTALL

LOVE AND LIES

Complete and Unabridged

LINFORD
Leicester

First published in Great Britain in 2019

First Linford Edition
published 2020

A catalogue record for this book is available from the British Library.

ISBN 978-1-4448-4488-7

Published by
Ulverscroft Limited
Anstey, Leicestershire

Set by Words & Graphics Ltd.
Anstey, Leicestershire
Printed and bound in Great Britain by
T. J. International Ltd., Padstow, Cornwall

This book is printed on acid-free paper

Prologue:
July 1976

Rosie looked out from the hilltop over the hazy fields bursting with myriad shades of yellow, brown and green. She closed her eyes and gave in to the drowsiness. Would this heat never end?

She gently removed a couple of ladybirds from her thin cotton top, then lay back languidly on the dry grass under the shade of a beech tree and sighed, fanning herself with a dog-eared paperback copy of 'Tess Of The d'Urbervilles'.

He had said he would ring this evening.

The Interview: Autumn 1975

'I had no idea the drive would be this long!'

Rosie pulled her navy blue shoulder bag a little closer to her body and lengthened her stride. It wouldn't do to be late for the interview.

'This must be it here, round the bend. Oh, I see, there's still quite a long way to go but at least the school is in sight now.'

Rosie stepped this way and that to avoid the potholes in the road. Several times she had to dodge quickly to the side as ripe chestnuts flung themselves down from the canopy of trees, their prickly cases threatening to scratch her as they flew past.

'I didn't expect this,' she said aloud. 'You trees, behave yourselves! I reckon the drive is at least a mile long. I suppose when they said it was a short distance to the school from the front gates, they meant a short journey in a car.'

Rosie had taken the bus — several buses, in fact, for Shaston Convent School was a rambling, long and roundabout sort of journey by public transport from her home in Bath. The last bus she had taken had deposited her at the end of the school drive a good ten minutes ago.

'Want a lift? It's beginning to rain and you don't want to arrive soaked to the skin, do you? Not for an interview.'

Rosie stared into the red MG sports car that had stopped beside her. Was she dreaming? The occupant of the car looked the closest she had ever seen to the Greek god Apollo, or at least how she imagined he would look if he suddenly appeared in Dorset in 1975.

The apparition had a satisfyingly well-balanced chiselled nose and piercing blue eyes. His manly hands grasped the steering wheel lightly.

'You look as if you've seen a ghost! Sorry to startle you. Come on, hop in. The wind's whipping up.'

'How did you know I was going to the school for an interview? I'm . . . '

'Rosie Peach, yes, I know. And I'm David Hart. Pleased to meet you. That's it, always seems a bit lower than you expect when you get into a sports car but you get used to it. You do know you've got a horse chestnut case stuck in your hair, don't you? I'll help you to get rid of it. That's better.

'Now, to explain the mystery of how I know you're Miss Rosie Peach,' he continued, 'I'm on the staff at Shaston and I take the choirs, teach a few music lessons, play the organ in chapel, that sort of thing.

'I knew as soon as I saw you in the drive you must be coming for your interview for the piano teaching job. I can always spot a pianist!'

'How?' Rosie raised her eyebrows quizzically and then laughed as David shook his head and refused to answer, tapping the side of his nose instead.

'Here we are then — Shaston Convent School. Good luck! I'm sure you'll get the job. Ring the bell over there and someone will let you in. I'm off to park my car round the back.'

Rosie clambered out and looked round in amazement at the imposing building in front of her. How could this be a school? It looked more like a stately home open to the public.

As she walked towards the heavy oak door with its Gothic metal bell pull on the right, several girls stuck their heads out of windows high up on the side wing of the building.

'Mr Hart! Mr Hart!' they chorused to the departing MG, then blew extravagant kisses into the crisp autumnal air.

It's like St Trinian's, Rosie thought, highly amused. What have I let myself in for?

She pulled the bell. While waiting for the door to open, she looked down the drive and was amazed to see what appeared to be a driverless Mini racing towards her.

It wasn't until the car was quite close that Rosie could see there was a diminutive nun at the steering wheel. It was a wonder she could see out of the windscreen.

The grandiose front door began to open very slowly, with much creaking.

'I saw you arrive with Mr Hart, my dear,' a striking figure said. 'You are most welcome. Come in, please. I'm Sister Anthony. You must be Miss Peach? I trust you had a pleasant journey?'

Rosie nodded.

'Yes, thank you.'

'Good.' Sister Anthony grinned. 'I'm going to take you to the blue parlour for a nice cup of tea.'

Rosie followed Sister Anthony into the large entrance hall lit by an enormous window over a fine wide staircase leading up to countless other rooms.

The highly polished floors and honey-coloured panelled walls gave off the fragrant smell of beeswax. Sister Anthony showed her into a light and airy room with celestial blue walls, and a stunning view of the grounds and endless countryside beyond.

'Oh, it's beautiful!' Rosie exclaimed. 'I can see why it's called the blue parlour.'

'Blue as a perfect summer's day,' Sister Anthony agreed.

'Such a wonderful lawn, too.' Rosie looked through the floor-length windows to the grass beyond. 'The girls must have so much fun running around there.'

'The girls aren't allowed on the nuns' lawn, my dear. They have plenty of other places to let off steam.'

Sister Anthony limped towards the door of the parlour.

'Please, do sit down, Miss Peach. I'll send your tea in shortly. In the meantime maybe you'd like to read some of our school magazines? Help yourself from the table. There are some lovely pictures of the old girls' weddings at the back.'

Rosie picked up a copy of the 'Shaston Chronicle' from the round polished table and examined a few of the black and white wedding photographs showing smiling young women dressed in long milkmaid-style Laura Ashley frocks, clinging on to the arms of nervous looking young men.

'Lovely dresses,' she murmured.

Looking around the room in awe, she noticed a shiny black upright piano against the far wall.

'Bechstein,' she said in delight as she lifted the lid of the instrument and saw the famous manufacturer's name picked out in gold above the keyboard. 'My favourite.'

Unable to resist tinkling the ivories, Rosie sat down and began to play a dreamy Chopin waltz.

'How lovely,' a voice said. 'Please don't stop.'

Rosie spun round on the leather

covered piano stool to see a tall elegant robed figure at the door.

'I'm Reverend Mother. We are so glad you want to join us and help our girls to appreciate music.

'Here, I've brought you some tea. The headmistress will see you in a little while, but I thought I would come and sit with you in case you have any questions about the school, and of course I would love you to tell me about yourself.'

Reverend Mother was a very good listener. Rosie told her all about her three years at college in London studying music and how she had now returned to live with her parents in Bath and was looking for her first job.

'Where would you live if you worked here, Miss Peach? Bath is quite a long way to travel every day.'

'Especially by public transport,' Rosie agreed, 'and I had no idea the drive would be so long. Luckily I had a lift for the last bit.'

'Yes, I gather you have already met

our Mr Hart.' Reverend Mother fixed Rosie with beady eyes.

'I would look for a room to rent in a house in Shaston, in the town,' Rosie said, 'if I were lucky enough to be offered the job, that is.'

Sister Anthony reappeared at the door.

'The headmistress will see you now, Miss Peach. Please follow me.'

In no time at all, Rosie was sitting in front of Sister Francis, the headmistress, being quizzed about her own education, her hopes for the future, any teaching experience and how she would deal with pupils who were reluctant to practise.

'We have found that some of our girls are naturally inclined to slackness in their practice sessions — indeed, in everything they do — and we are looking for a teacher who can inspire them. Do you think you are that person, Miss Peach?'

'I . . . I hope so,' Rosie said. 'I will try to be. I absolutely love music and especially the piano, and would hope to communicate that to my pupils.'

'How?'

'By playing to them and listening to them, choosing pieces that suit them and that they like. I always play with my pupils, too, lots of duet playing, then, of course, ensemble playing, and concerts, informal and formal, festivals, competitions . . . '

Rosie tried to slow down, suspecting she was beginning to gabble.

'Exactly how many pupils have you taught, Miss Peach?'

'Quite a good number, actually,' Rosie said, more sure of her ground now. 'I used to teach when I was in the sixth form at school, to help save up the money I needed to buy music and for my own lessons.

'Then when I was at college I taught ten pupils a week to help with the money towards my rent and living expenses. Oh, and I played for ballet classes on Saturdays.'

'I see,' Sister Francis said. 'That is

admirable. Your parents must be very proud of you.'

Rosie kept her fingers crossed for good luck the whole time she was being interviewed because she had already decided there was nothing she wanted more than to work at Shaston School.

Sister Francis stood up and offered Rosie her hand.

'Thank you, Miss Peach, that will be all for now. We will be in touch, but before you go, I have arranged for our head girl and her deputy to take you on a tour of the school and then you will have the opportunity to meet Miss Spiker, one of our longest standing instrumental teachers.

'We greatly value the contribution she has made to the artistic life of the school.

'She wants to cut down the amount of teaching she does with a view to retiring in the not too distant future and whoever gets the job will be working closely with her, under her guidance and maybe in time helping to relieve her of some of her teaching burden.

'She has been here a very long time and would benefit from working with someone, how can I put it? More energetic and . . . '

'Up to date,' Sister Anthony said, suddenly appearing at the door. 'Have you mentioned Miss Spiker's artistic temperament?'

'I didn't think that was necessary,' Sister Francis said. 'Miss Peach has been to music college. She is fully aware how temperamental and easily offended musicians can be.'

'Fair enough.' Sister Anthony smiled at Rosie. 'The girls are ready to take you round the school now.'

'Thank you, Sister Anthony.' Sister Francis gave a gracious nod of her head. 'Goodbye, Miss Peach. I hope you have enjoyed your visit to Shaston and I hope, too, that we will see you again.'

'She liked you,' one of the girls confided to Rosie as they showed her round the lower school classrooms.

'Really?' Rosie asked. 'How do you know?'

'She was smiling,' the other girl said. 'That's rare, for Sister Frowncis.'

Both girls started to giggle until Rosie felt she had to say something or she herself might feel compelled to join in.

'So, tell me about yourselves. How long have you both been at the school? You'll have to remind me of your names, too, as I'm afraid I've forgotten.'

'I'm Lucy and I've been here since I was eight. I'm doing my A levels this year, worse luck.'

'Me too, but at least it means we'll soon be out of here. I'm Arabella and I started when I was six. I can't wait to leave and get on with life.'

'Not that we don't like it, of course,' Lucy hastily assured Rosie.

'The teachers aren't too bad, on the whole,' Arabella said, 'and we can go riding on Saturdays.'

'We're allowed to watch television on

Sunday afternoons, if we ask Sister Francis first and show her the programme details in the 'Radio Times',' Lucy said.

'Best of all, though,' Arabella added, 'is now we're in the sixth form we're allowed to have showers.'

'Yes, lower down the school it's two baths a week and hair wash once a week.' Lucy held her nose.

'Goodness,' Rosie said, beginning to feel rather sorry for the girls at Shaston.

'Would you like to see the sixth form block?' Arabella asked. 'We have study bedrooms.'

'Sounds good,' Rosie replied. 'So you don't all have to sleep in long dormitories?'

'Oh, no,' Lucy said. 'The little ones sleep in the large dormitories and the Lower Fours and Upper Fives sleep in Slum Alley.'

'Where?' Rosie thought she must have misheard.

'Slum Alley,' Arabella said. 'It's in the oldest part of the school and the rooms are tiny with uneven bumpy floorboards and four iron beds crammed into each room. We're not encouraged to show visitors that part of the school.'

'There was a rat there once,' Lucy said. 'It died under the floorboards and the whole place stank for ages afterwards. Oh, I've just remembered — we're not meant to talk about Slum Alley and the rat, not to visitors.'

Lucy's face contorted with the effort of not giving way to rising hysteria and Arabella cleared her throat loudly then burst into fits of laughter.

'Maybe you could show me the music department?' Rosie suggested. 'I'm due to meet Miss Spiker there in ten minutes.'

'Lead on, Macduff,' Lucy said as Arabella strode outside, through a courtyard, past the front door and down a steep path round the back of a massive hall with impressive turrets and an enormous bay window.

'The hall used to be a ballroom,' Arabella said, 'when the school was a grand country house.'

'Here's where the music takes place,' Lucy said as the three of them approached a low grey hut behind the hall. It seemed to Rosie a bit like one of the wartime prefabs that still existed near her home in Bath.

'Goodness,' Rosie marvelled once she was inside the main room. 'This is like a tiny bit of Austria, in the middle of Dorset. Mozart would feel quite at home here. Look at all those instruments and the beautiful pictures and craft work.'

'Reverend Mother embroidered the cushions herself, after she came back from a visit to Salzburg with the school choir.' Lucy picked up one of the colourful creations and handed it to Rosie for her to have a closer look.

'Super needlework,' Rosie said. 'Reverend Mother is very talented. You girls are lucky to have such a beautiful music room to have your lessons in.' She sat down on one of the cosy benches and smiled.

'Miss Spiker used to teach me the piano when I was a Junior,' Arabella said, 'but sadly I was totally useless. She used to have to tap my fingers with her ruler because they kept playing the wrong notes.'

'Only because you were too lazy to practise,' Lucy said.

'You have to practise, that's for sure,' Rosie agreed. 'What about you, Lucy? Are you fond of music?'

'Yes, I sing in the chapel choir and I learn the piano with Miss Spiker. Look, there, out of the window. There's Miss Spiker coming to meet you.'

'This is where we leave you,' Arabella said.

'Thank you so much, girls,' Rosie said. 'I feel I've had a unique insight into the life of the school listening to your tales.'

'We'll be late for lunch if we don't scarper,' Lucy warned.

'Goodbye, Miss Peach,' the girls called as they ran off.

Rosie sprang to her feet as Miss

Spiker came into the room.

'Miss Peach, I presume?' she rasped. 'Have you had a good look round? Sort of place you like, is it? I will be keeping all my pupils, whatever you have heard. Your job will be to teach the beginners then hand the good ones on to me.'

Miss Spiker stood in front of Rosie, glaring at her quite fiercely. Her eyebrows were pencilled in as wafer thin arches, higher than eyebrows usually are, and a scarlet mouth was drawn on her powdered face, not exactly following the outline of her lips.

Her hair gave the appearance of having been styled with an egg whisk.

'That, that sounds good.' Rosie clenched her teeth together.

'Speak up, girl! Speak up! Can't abide mumblers and mutterers. What's that you said?'

'I only said it sounded good.' Rosie looked at the floor, her confidence deserting her. How would she be able to work with Miss Spiker? Maybe it wasn't the right job after all?

'Play me something,' Miss Spiker commanded.

Rosie sat down at the piano and began playing a slow sad lament, her fingers missing a few notes as her hands shook.

'Now something fast,' the order came.

Rosie duly obliged and rattled off a Scott Joplin Rag.

'Mmm. At least you can play.' Miss Spiker paced around the room. 'You'll be answerable to me, understand? No-one else.'

Rosie nodded, not sure what else to do, then decided to pull herself together. She was sure Miss Spiker would welcome her thoughts on how to develop the department.

'Miss Spiker, I wonder, would you mind if I started a few initiatives of my own? If I get the job, of course. Perhaps I could take the girls out to local music festivals and organise some concerts for them at the weekends? Things like that?

'I was talking to Sister Francis about

it in my interview and she thought it sounded like a good idea, to open out the opportunities for the girls, as they have a lot of free time on their hands and maybe need a bit more direction in their musical studies.'

'Nonsense! The girls are fully occupied and we compete in an annual music festival already. I'm surprised you haven't bothered to find out about it.

'There will be no time for extra 'initiatives' and 'direction'. As I have already said, you will be answerable to me. Understood? That is, if you get the job.'

'I apologise if I have overstepped the mark in any way. Please believe me, I meant no harm and I am willing to work as part of a team.'

Wow, Rosie thought. I'm beginning to realise the challenges of this post.

'What about another cup of tea?' Sister Anthony asked as she limped into the room. 'Sister Francis and Reverend Mother would be pleased to receive you both in the blue parlour for a final meeting.'

'Are there scones?' Miss Spiker demanded. 'I usually have scones.'

'There are indeed,' Sister Anthony said in a reassuring voice.

'And may I, er, may I . . . ' Rosie started.

'I'll show you where the cloakroom is,' Sister Anthony said. 'No doubt you'd like to freshen up.'

Rosie stared at herself in a large foxed mirror hung over the basin of the visitors' wash-room, glad of the opportunity to be alone for a few minutes. She regarded her unruly hair critically as it threatened to burst out of the chignon she had twisted it into for her visit to the convent in an attempt to look older.

She ran her hands under the tap for a few seconds, then dabbed at a few over-enthusiastic strands to try to tame them.

'Bother!' she said to her reflection.

'Looks even worse, if that's possible.

Still, I don't suppose the nuns judge by appearance — let's hope not, anyway.'

Hastily sweeping on a slick of pink lipstick, she rushed out into the corridor where Sister Anthony was yet again waiting to escort her to her destination, the final meeting in the blue parlour over tea and scones.

* * *

By the time Rosie arrived back at her parents' house in Bath she was totally exhausted.

'Eat up, love,' Sheila, Rosie's mother, urged. 'I made shepherd's pie especially.'

'My favourite! Thanks, Mum.'

'Yes,' Rosie's father, Brian, said, 'eat up and then carry on with what happened next. We've got as far as tea in the blue parlour. What did everyone say? Was that Miss Spiker any friendlier?'

'Well,' Rosie said, 'we had a delicious tea, not only scones but sandwiches and cake, all sorts of treats — and yes, Miss Spiker was a lot nicer in front of the nuns. She smiled at me and said she was sure I'd do a grand job. Bit odd, really.'

'What about your journey back?' Sheila asked. 'Did that handsome young music teacher give you another lift down the drive?'

'Mum!' Rosie said. 'I wish I'd never told you about him. But that was a bit odd, too. He drove past me as I was walking to the bus stop at the end of the drive and I waved at him.

'I didn't expect him to stop and offer me a lift because he already had a passenger, but he didn't even slow down or smile, nothing at all. He had quite a serious look, actually.'

'Who was his passenger?' Brian asked.

'Miss Spiker.'

'Never mind, dear. Now, I've got some lovely stewed apple for you. Custard?' Sheila bustled about, getting the pudding assembled.

'Will you take the job, if they offer it to you?' Brian asked.

'My first thought is yes, but I might have changed my mind by tomorrow. They said they'd write, anyway, not telephone, so I've got time to mull over whether I can work with someone who is, how shall I put it, slightly hostile? I loved the school, though, and the girls were truly delightful. That probably counts for much more, doesn't it?'

Rosie stood up and yawned.

'I think I'll have a bath and early night, maybe read my book in bed. Thanks for a lovely meal, Mum.'

'I'll bring you up some cocoa in a while.'

'Perfect.'

* * *

As Rosie relaxed in bed that night, she thought over the day. Fancy someone like me going for an interview at Shaston School, she reflected.

It's another world, a world of

privilege — and the setting is amazing, with acres of countryside all around and the long drive with chestnut trees and rhododendron bushes. Why, it must be an absolute picture in the summer.

Mind you, the girls had some stories to tell, about Slum Alley and the rat. They don't seem to have much freedom, either. Maybe not such a place of privilege after all.

Rosie's last conscious thought before drifting off to sleep was the thrilling memory of how David Hart had gently removed the chestnut case from her hair earlier that day.

He had dislodged the spiky intruder then smoothed a few flyaway strands of her hair back, all the while gazing at her intensely with his meltingly attractive blue eyes.

A New Adventure

Rosie cycled to work on her first day at Shaston School, her leather music case balanced precariously in the wicker basket over the front wheel.

The last week had been a complete whirlwind.

I wouldn't have managed without Mum and Dad's help, Rosie thought as she bowled down the drive, enjoying the fresh air whipping through her hair. They've been brilliant. They always are.

The letter offering Rosie the post of 'Teacher of Pianoforte' at Shaston Convent School had arrived in the first post of the day, two days after her interview, and Rosie's father Brian had joked that Sister Francis must have written it as soon as the interview finished, if not before.

'That's my girl,' he had said proudly. 'Your first full-time job! I knew the nuns would recognise your talent and potential.'

Rosie had smiled and pointed out that she didn't think anyone else had applied for the job.

'And besides, I need to consider whether I really want to take it. Interviews are two-way processes.'

'Think carefully, Rosie,' her mother had advised. 'You did have some reservations about working with Miss Spiker.'

'I know,' Rosie said, 'but I think I can handle any difficulties.'

Besides, she added to herself, I'll be able to see David Hart again. I'm sure he didn't mean to ignore me when he passed after my interview. He was probably too busy chatting to Miss Spiker.

'I'm going to take the job,' Rosie had said confidently to her parents, the decision made. 'They've asked me to ring straight away as they need someone to start as soon as possible.'

Rosie reached the end of the drive

and cycled past the front door she had used when she had come for her interview.

She followed the path across the front of the refectory where she could see hordes of girls tucking into their breakfast, through the arch of the clock tower, across a courtyard and round to the back of the laundry building where there was a shed for staff to put their bicycles.

It had taken her about twenty minutes to cycle in from her lodgings in Shaston.

'Another thing to be grateful to Mum and Dad for,' she murmured. 'They not only found a place for me to stay with what a really nice family, but they even paid the first month's rent and deposit for me.'

'Miss Peach. Welcome!' A tiny nun stood in front of Rosie, her lively face wreathed in a huge smile. 'I'm Sister Anne and I work in the laundry.'

'Hello,' Rosie said. 'I think I might have seen you driving a Mini on the day

I came for interview? Pleased to meet you.'

Rosie wondered how Sister Anne had managed to appear so silently and how much she had heard of her monologue.

'You've got very special parents, I think,' Sister Anne said.

Ah, Rosie thought. She heard quite a lot. I've got the feeling this is a place where everyone knows everything about everybody else.

'Yes, I have.' Rosie smiled.

'You'll be wanting someone to guide you to the staffroom, I think. Here's Sister Anthony. Have a good day, Miss Peach.'

As Sister Anne scurried away, Sister Anthony limped forward, ready to escort Rosie into the building.

'This way, my dear.'

'Thank you,' Rosie said. 'I was wondering how I would find my way around. There are so many doors into the building and so many corridors to get lost in.'

'You'll soon feel at home,' Sister

Anthony reassured her.

'Sister Francis will have a quick word with you in the staff room then you've got your first pupil at nine-thirty. We're all very keen to know how you both get on.'

* * *

To Rosie's delight, her first piano pupil was Lucy, one of the sixth formers who had showed her around on her interview day.

'How lovely to see you, Lucy,' Rosie said, 'but I thought you said you were having lessons with Miss Spiker?'

'Miss Spiker has given up with me,' Lucy said with a laugh. 'I asked too many questions, I think. Shall I play you a piece?'

Within minutes Lucy and Rosie were immersed in a Chopin nocturne, sorting out the intricacies of semi-quaver runs and subtle pedalling, and then, too soon for both of them, the lesson was over.

In the staff room at break, Rosie helped herself to a cup of tea from an enormous catering-sized tea pot.

She noticed Miss Spiker sitting on the other side of the room, chatting to colleagues, but decided not to disturb her.

Miss Spiker seemed to be holding court, jabbing her finger every so often and casting unfriendly looks in Rosie's direction.

'How's it all going?' David Hart came up to Rosie as she stood looking out of the window at the beautiful countryside, wondering whether she had made the right decision coming to work at Shaston School.

'Fabulous view, isn't it?' David said. 'Thomas Hardy country, one of the best bits of England, in my opinion. Have a biscuit — all lovingly made by the team of Irish nuns in the kitchen.

'For this reason alone, Shaston School is a wonderful place to work.'

David held a plate of the delicious homemade creations in front of Rosie and she helped herself to a large, rustic-looking biscuit bulging with nuts and chunks of chocolate.

'Thank you,' she said. 'It's going fine; I've just given Lucy a piano lesson.'

'Lucy? But I thought . . . ' David started to say. 'I mean, it's none of my business but . . . '

'What is it?' Rosie said through a mouthful of biscuit. 'Anything wrong? We had a great lesson — lovely Chopin piece.'

'Miss Spiker said she didn't want to stop teaching Lucy,' David explained. 'I mean she is, or rather was, one of her best pupils. How come she's learning with you, if you don't mind me asking?'

'I . . . I don't really know,' Rosie stuttered anxiously. 'When I saw Sister Francis this morning she said I was to teach her, and Lucy herself said Miss Spiker didn't want to teach her any more as she asked too many questions.

'Oh dear, I hope I haven't messed up on my first day here. I don't want to upset Miss Spiker.'

'Leave it with me,' David said grimly. 'I think I know what's going on — Miss Spiker is displaying her famous temperament.

'We all think she's marvellous but she does have a bit of a reputation for being difficult. In fact, she's well known for it. If my suspicions are correct, you're owed an apology, not least from me.'

David gave Rosie a sympathetic look.

'Not a pleasant start for you, a muddle like this on your very first day. I'll try to catch you at lunchtime and let you know what's happening. You're coming to play for the choir, aren't you?'

'Yes,' Rosie said. 'I'm a bit nervous but I've been practising the piano accompaniment. I don't want to let you down.'

'I can't ever imagine that happening,' David said softly. 'Oh, and by the way, you might have a surprise when you meet your next pupil. See you later and don't worry about Miss Spiker.'

Rosie's heart beat a little faster as she

hurried along the sweet-smelling corridors to her next lesson. So there is something a bit odd about Miss Spiker and her attitude to me, she mused.

She hoped David could sort it out soon. She didn't want any unpleasantness.

At the thought of David Hart, Rosie's own heart did a little somersault. He really was terribly good-looking in an old-fashioned, romantic sort of way.

Goodness, he could be cast in a film adaptation of a Thomas Hardy book, Rosie was sure. And to think he was one of her colleagues . . .

When Rosie got to her teaching room, she found a young girl with strawberry blonde hair sitting at the piano with a book open in front of her.

'Shall I play you my minuet?' the girl asked cheerfully.

Rosie thought the girl reminded her of someone, but she couldn't quite place it.

'I'm Clementine,' the small girl continued. 'Clementine Morgan-Hart and I'm doing my Grade One soon. I'm six.'

Of course, Rosie thought. David. She looks like David, but that means David must be married, with a family, too.

'So, are you related to Mr Hart?' Rosie asked.

'Of course!' Clementine said. 'What a funny question. He often takes me home but sometimes Mummy takes me home. I'm not a boarder because we only live in the next village. I can play all my scales. Shall I start now?'

'Fire away,' Rosie said. 'Let's warm up with G major scale, then you can play your minuet.'

Rosie tried very hard to concentrate in the lesson but her brain was on fire with all sorts of questions. Why hadn't David told her about Clementine?

But he did, a small voice in Rosie's head said. At least, he said you would have a surprise.

Why didn't I realise he was married, Rosie wondered. She even thought perhaps David hadn't quite behaved as if he was married and that confused her. He had been flirting with her.

Was he indeed, the small voice in her head continued, or were you being a silly naïve girl and imagining all sorts of things?

No, I wasn't, Rosie thought crossly. He definitely gave me the impression he, well, he . . .

'Miss Peach? Shall we finish now? The bell's gone and I've got Art next; it's my favourite subject,' Clementine said as she closed her books, hastily adding, 'next to piano, of course.'

'Yes. See you next week, Clementine. I'm sure you'll finish the piece I gave you easily, but if you have any difficulty, you can ask at home for help, can't you?'

'Oh, yes,' Clementine said. 'I can get a lot of help at home.'

* * *

Lunch in the refectory was shockingly noisy, with chairs scraped carelessly along the hard floor, serving spoons clattering on the metal dishes and the babble of voices rising ever higher.

Rosie stood at the door and tried in vain to see where she should sit.

Sister Francis had said she was welcome to have school lunch but she couldn't see any other teachers sitting down, just a couple of members of staff wandering between the tables reminding the girls to keep the noise down, while Sister Anne and two other nuns staggered backwards and forwards from the kitchen with huge plates of food.

'There you are,' David said. 'Glad I've found you. Are you on lunch duty? On your first day here?'

'No. I thought this was where I would have my lunch.'

David shuddered.

'The thought of eating with this rabble isn't pleasant,' he said. 'We have our own staff dining-room. I think Miss Spiker was supposed to make sure you knew where to go after your morning's teaching.'

'I haven't seen her at all,' Rosie said.

'Why am I not surprised to hear that? Come on, I'll show you where the dining-room is. Come and have lunch with me, then we can have a coffee in the blue parlour afterwards.

'We won't be disturbed there and I can tell you what's been going on.'

* * *

David and Rosie enjoyed a delicious lunch with other teaching colleagues in the civilised surroundings of the staff dining-room, then, as promised, David explained everything over coffee in the blue parlour.

'Do you take milk, Rosie?' he asked. 'Now, down to business.'

Rosie looked at David anxiously while she clutched her coffee cup.

'I've found out that Miss Spiker has been a little economical with the truth,' David said. 'She has been going round saying you're pushing her aside and trying to take over her department, the department she's built up over many years.'

'You mean she's been lying?' Rosie said indignantly.

'That's the long and the short of it, yes,' David said. 'I told you she could be difficult. She resents your appointment and has accused you, most unfairly I now realise, of empire building.'

Rosie gave a sharp intake of breath. Empire building was about the worst thing one teacher could accuse another of.

'But I've only been here one morning,' Rosie said. 'It would be hard to build an empire that quickly.'

'Quite,' David said. 'It's nonsensical. And listen to this, when you saw Miss Spiker this morning in the staff room with her coven around her, I mean her colleagues, she was telling them you had poached Lucy, her best piano pupil, but the truth is she herself set the whole situation up by telling Lucy she didn't want to teach her any more, so

Sister Francis put Lucy down on your list of pupils.'

Rosie's hand flew to her mouth.

'Whatever shall I do?'

'You don't have to do anything,' David said, frowning. 'I've been to see Sister Francis and the truth will soon filter around the staff.

'You'll probably find quite a few colleagues will come up to you now and start being super friendly because they feel a bit guilty for listening to her nonsense. I know I feel like that.

'So sorry, Rosie,' he continued, 'I nearly believed Miss Spiker at first, too. I gave her a lift home on the day of your interview and she told me a few things about you that I now know were silly exaggerations and misrepresentations.'

David put his hand over Rosie's and there was silence between them.

'Thank you for sorting it all out,' Rosie said.

'No problem.'

David face lit up with a lovely warm smile and Rosie felt goosebumps travelling down her back, until she suddenly remembered that David was only being kind, nothing more. After all, he had a perfect family waiting for him at home, didn't he?

'Can you hear that noise?' David asked.

It was hard to miss what sounded like a small army careering past the blue parlour.

'That's the choir. They've finished their lunch and had a run around outside. Now they're on the way to the hall for our rehearsal.'

'We'd better get cracking then,' Rosie said. 'Full steam ahead. Messiah here we come!'

'Before you go,' a small voice said, 'I wondered if I might have a word, Miss Peach.'

Rosie gasped when she saw Miss Spiker standing at the door of the blue parlour.

'Perhaps you would do the vocal warm-ups with the choir, Mr Hart? I won't be long and Miss Peach will be able to join you in a minute.'

As David hurried off, Miss Spiker closed the door firmly, much to the annoyance of Sister Anne and Sister Anthony who were lurking in the corridor.

'I'm so sorry, my dear Miss Peach — Rosie, if I may call you that,' she said, twisting a delicate lace handkerchief in her fingers.

'I've been a foolish old woman and a jealous one too. I am full of shame for my behaviour. Please forgive me.

'Your first day here should have been a joy but I've spoiled it for you and I was even foul to you when you came to your interview because I thought it would put you off.

'The truth is, I know it's nearly time for me to retire. The nuns have been very patient and accommodating but I really need someone to help me shoulder the load now. Will you be that person? Can we start again? Could we be friends?'

'Of course, Miss Spiker,' Rosie said

with a beaming smile. 'It will be a pleasure.'

Miss Spiker beamed back.

'Please call me Dorcas, my dear. You are too generous and I don't deserve it. Now you must run along to choir.'

As Rosie opened the door, Sister Anne sprang to her feet.

'Just polishing the floor,' she said.

I can't wait to ring my parents tonight and tell them all about this, Rosie thought, highly amused. What a relief all the unpleasantness is over.

* * *

Ten minutes later, she was playing the beautiful grand piano in the hall with rows of girls singing their hearts out as David conducted.

'Hallelujah! Hallelujah!'

'Wonderful,' David called out. 'Plenty of breath for this last phrase . . . '

The girls raised the roof as they sang Handel's mighty 'Hallelujah Chorus'. When the music ended, the echoes bounced around the worn wooden floor and peeling walls, and the stained glass in the massive bay window twinkled as the autumn sunshine lit up the room.

'Thank you, Miss Peach,' David said to Rosie. 'Girls — a round of applause for your new accompanist.'

Lucy stood up to lead the applause for Rosie.

'Miss Peach! Miss Peach!' several girls called out, whooping with excitement.

I'm going to enjoy my work here, Rosie thought as she acknowledged the girls' applause.

* * *

By the time Rosie had cycled back to her lodgings, she felt in need of a strong cup of tea.

'Hello, Rosie,' Mrs Field said as Rosie stumbled through the front door.

There were shoes and coats scattered all over the floor of the hall and three satchels hanging on the banisters.

Sounds of shrieking and laughter could be heard from the garden where Mrs Field's children were playing.

'Did you have a good day? I forgot to say yesterday when you arrived that you're very welcome to use the telephone whenever you want — please don't hesitate. And if there's anything else you need, give me a shout.'

'Thanks,' Rosie answered. 'I think I will make a quick call to my mother. She worries about me.'

'Goes with the job description,' Mrs Field said as she melted away to the kitchen to give Rosie some privacy.

Sheila answered the phone after the first ring.

'How did it go, Rosie? We've been thinking about you such a lot today.'

Rosie told her about the events of the day.

'Fancy Miss Spiker being friendly after all and how amazing her first name is Dorcas,' her mother said.

'She's a good sort underneath,' Rosie said. 'I'm putting it down to the artistic temperament Sister Anthony mentioned at my interview. And it takes guts to apologise like that.'

'Takes guts to accept an apology too,' Sheila said. 'You're very generous, Rosie. Artistic temperament? Excuse for bad behaviour, more likely. At least you don't suffer from an artistic temperament and aren't easily offended.

'Now, I mustn't keep you, but before I go, what are you having for supper? Have you got plenty of food? Have you unpacked all your belongings yet?'

'Mum!' Rosie said. 'I have been away from home before. And yes, I have got something to eat for supper, thank you, and I've unpacked. I did all that yesterday.

'There are quite a few shops near the Fields' house, including a supermarket. The food cupboard is bulging.'

'Sorry, Rosie,' Sheila said. 'It's hard to accept you're grown up sometimes. You'll find out when you have your own children. Bye, darling. Speak soon.'

Rosie's supper consisted of pilchards on toast and an apple. She was far too shattered to manage either to cook or to eat anything more complicated.

She spent some time getting everything ready for the next day of her great adventure. First she sorted out the music she needed, then pulled various items of clothing out of the wardrobe, changing her mind about her outfit several times before she felt confident she had made the right choice.

Sitting by the gas fire in her room wearing her dressing-gown, Rosie mulled over the day.

I'm lucky to have this job, she thought, but if only, if only David were single . . .

Playing Cupid

David Hart hummed as he drove to school. Things were definitely looking up. First of all, he was pleased he had been able to sort out the business with Miss Spiker and Rosie to everyone's satisfaction.

He admired Rosie for being so forgiving and admired Miss Spiker, too, for being honest in the end and apologising for her behaviour.

It couldn't be easy, David thought, to realise your career as a musician was drawing to a close, especially with Miss Spiker being single as well.

Suddenly David's mood changed and he shifted uncomfortably in his car seat, thinking of his mother's words to him the previous weekend when he had visited her for a scrumptious Sunday lunch.

'David,' she had asked, 'have you met

anyone special recently? Isn't it about time you found yourself a nice young lady?

'After all, it's been three years now since your Donna passed away. She'd want you to find someone else, to be happy, don't you think?'

David thumped the steering wheel in exasperation. His mother didn't understand, had never understood. It was pointless trying to explain things to her and besides, he didn't want to talk about Donna to anyone.

'What about that young piano teacher who's joined the staff?' his mother had persisted. 'Is she attached?'

'Mum,' David had said, 'if I choose to go out with anyone, or choose to marry again, it won't only be because they are single and have joined the music staff at Shaston School.'

David crashed the gears as he sped round a tight bend in the lane.

I'm not ready for all that again, he thought. Not after Donna. A sudden vision of Rosie sprang into his mind, her eyes dancing merrily as she smiled at him. No, he thought, however tempting Rosie Peach is, I can't contemplate anything like that.

* * *

Arriving at work, he bumped into Reverend Mother in the car park.

'Hello, Mr Hart! I'm so looking forward to the excursion to Salisbury Cathedral next week. How are the preparations going?'

'All under control.' David smiled. He had organised a trip to hear 'Bach's B Minor Mass' for the girls next Wednesday evening and Reverend Mother was as keen as mustard to attend.

'Bach is my favourite composer, you know,' Reverend Mother continued.

'Mine too,' David said. 'It's such a glorious piece, isn't it?'

'I've asked Miss Peach to join us,' Reverend Mother continued, 'as one of the Upper Five has come down with tonsillitis, poor lamb, and that left us with a spare ticket.'

'Oh, er, great,' David said. 'It'll be good to have another adult on the coach, to help supervise the girls. They can be quite a handful when they get over excited.'

'And she's a musician to boot,' Reverend Mother replied. 'Lovely young woman, Miss Peach. Make someone an excellent wife one day, no doubt.'

David wasn't sure but he thought Reverend Mother actually winked at him when she said this. Good heavens, was there no end to the scheming of women?

'Must dash,' David said, taking the chance to scuttle away from matrimonial discussions. 'Music festival for the choir to organise — paperwork's due in soon.'

'Of course,' Reverend Mother said. 'I won't detain you any longer. Have a good day.'

By lunchtime, David had completed the entry form for the choir for the annual music festival and had chosen the programme the girls would be singing.

I'd better go and find Rosie, he said to himself, and give her the accompaniments.

He found her cradling a cup of tea in the staff room.

'Some music for you, Rosie,' he said. 'I think you know about the festival coming up soon?'

'Miss Spiker has told me all about it,' Rosie said. 'She's been so helpful. She didn't know who the adjudicator was, though.'

'Oh, it's a chap from London — can't quite remember his name. The festival information says he's a choral expert.'

'Whatever that means,' Rosie said with a laugh.

'Indeed,' David agreed. 'Now, what is his name? It's on the tip of my tongue: Tristan someone or other. Tristan Peacock?'

Rosie made a strange gurgling sound

as she nearly choked on her tea.

'Tristan?' She gulped. 'Not Tristan Proudfoot?'

'Do you know him?'

'I knew a Tristan Proudfoot at college. We were in the same year, students together.'

'Must be the same person,' David said. 'He's done well to get on the adjudicating circuit at his age, fresh from college. What's he like?'

'Very high musical standards.' Rosie burrowed in her handbag to hide her face. 'Just looking for a tissue,' she said. 'He could be slightly impatient and tricky, actually. Some people found him a bit of a pain. Tenacious sort of character.'

'Typical musician, then,' David joked but Rosie didn't join in with the laughter.

'Mustn't be late,' she said. 'Got to dash. See you at choir later.'

That was rather odd, David thought. How strange that Rosie knows the adjudicator. Still, the musical world can be very small. She didn't seem particularly keen to see him again, though.

* * *

Pupils and staff set off on their concert trip in high excitement the next Wednesday evening.

The girls had been allowed to dress in their own clothes instead of uniform for once and wore as much make-up as they could possibly get away with before they left the school, then applied more once hidden behind the tall red plush seats of the coach.

Arabella and Lucy, the two sixth formers who had originally shown Rosie round the school, sat right at the back with their friends.

'Don't worry about a thing, Miss Peach,' Arabella called out.

'Yes,' Lucy added. 'We'll keep an eye on the little ones.'

'I'm a prefect,' their friend Sophia said. 'I'll help Arabella and Lucy keep them quiet.'

'I doubt it,' David said, sitting at the front next to Reverend Mother. 'Those three are usually the noisiest and most badly behaved on the coach.'

'They like to let off steam,' Reverend Mother said serenely. 'It does them good. They'll soon quieten down.'

'Wouldn't bet on it,' David muttered, anticipating quite a lively evening.

'I wonder, Mr Hart, would you mind if I asked a favour?' Reverend Mother said.

'Of course not,' David replied. 'What is it?'

'I don't travel well and I think I'd be better off if I sat over there, where Miss Peach is sitting. You don't mind if she takes my place, do you?'

'Her seat is over the wheel,' David pointed out. 'Most people think that's a difficult place to sit if you feel queasy.'

'Not me,' Reverend Mother said. 'I prefer to sit on the wheel. I'm moving now. Miss Peach, please come and take my place.'

She's hell bent on pushing us

together, David thought. Perhaps she's in league with my mother?

Sister Anthony and Sister Anne seemed thrilled when Rosie moved to the seat next to David, directly in front of them.

'How come they're on the trip?' Rosie whispered.

'Two of the Lower Fours were taken off the list yesterday as a punishment,' David explained. 'They were caught running across the nuns' lawn in their dressing gowns after lights out.'

'That's very bad, obviously,' Rosie said, stifling a giggle. 'Shocking behaviour.'

Sister Anthony and Sister Anne leaned forward as one.

'So glad you two are getting on,' Sister Anne said.

'Yes,' Sister Anthony said, 'you are well suited.'

David held his head in his hands. It was going to be a long journey.

'Mr Hart! Mr Hart!' Lucy called out. 'I can see lights!'

'It's so exciting!' Sophia screeched.

'Hooray!' Arabella yelled. 'We're coming into the city.'

'So we are,' David said. 'Please stay in your seats, girls, and keep the noise down a bit. That's better.'

'It must seem terribly exciting to them,' Rosie said. 'They don't get out from school much.'

'Neither do the nuns,' David whispered. 'Look at Sister Anthony and Sister Anne behind us. They couldn't look more excited if they were on their way to Buckingham Palace to meet the Queen. You know they're actual sisters as well as both being nuns, don't you?'

'No,' Rosie said, 'but now you've told me I can see the resemblance. How sweet!'

'They're not sweet,' David said under his breath, a huge grin on his face. 'Don't let that act fool you. Reverend Mother's the same — ruthless and determined, more like.'

'They have made some pretty odd comments,' Rosie agreed. 'Not sure your wife would be too pleased.'

'My wife?' David's eyebrows shot up. 'I'm not married! That is, I . . . '

As they were getting off the coach near the beautiful close of Salisbury Cathedral, Sister Anthony sidled up to Rosie.

'Mr Hart is a widower.'

'Ah,' Rosie said, the light dawning along with a strange hopeful feeling right in the pit of her stomach. 'So Clementine, my pupil, he's bringing her up alone? He's a single parent? I'm sure she mentioned her mother, though.'

Sister Anne grabbed Rosie's arm.

'My dear,' she said, 'we thought you knew. Clementine Morgan-Hart is Mr Hart's niece. Mr Hart's sister, Isobel Hart, is married to Mr Morgan and Clementine is their daughter. They chose to put their names together as Morgan-Hart when they married.'

'I see,' Rosie said. 'So confusing, with a double-barrelled name.' Rosie suddenly realised that when Clementine had said David drove her home sometimes, it was obviously to save his sister the journey when it was practical for him.

'Mr Hart is very good with children,' Sister Anthony said. 'Very kind. He's had some sad times and he deserves to be happy.'

'Come along, girls,' David said. 'Time to take our seats.'

The party from Shaston joined the stream of music lovers on their way towards the magnificent cathedral, the girls subdued for once, overawed by the strangeness of being out of the convent.

Rosie looked up at the stone spire silhouetted against the starry sky way above them all.

Our worries are nothing, really, she thought, mere insignificant pinpricks in a glorious world.

She felt full of hope as she followed behind David, noticing his broad shoulders filling out his tweedy jacket.

The music was superb. At the end of the concert, as the dying chords hung between the ancient pillars before floating off into the vaulted ceiling, Rosie sneaked a look at David's face and was humbled to see he had tears in his eyes. She pressed her hand lightly on his sleeve.

'Beautiful, isn't it?'

'My wife Donna loved this piece,' David said. 'It brings back so many memories. Painful memories.'

Only a Kiss

The girls grew wild again on the coach as they returned to school, singing at the tops of their voices, changing seats frequently and drumming their feet on the floor until crisis point was reached. Spotting a lay-by, the poor coach driver screeched to a halt and leaped from his driving seat in a white hot rage.

'Now look 'ere,' he bellowed. 'You might think you're young ladies but I've never 'ad to put up with this behaviour before, truly I ain't.'

'We're always like this,' Arabella said.

'Yes,' Sophia remarked.

'Not true,' Lucy added. 'Sometimes we're much worse. Remember when . . . '

'Enough, girls,' David roared.

'Thank you, Mr Hart,' Reverend Mother said. 'I'll take it from here. Now, girls, what have you got to say to our coach driver?'

'May we stop for chips?' Arabella suggested.

'That would be lovely,' Sophia agreed.

'We are very, very sorry,' Lucy said. 'Aren't we, everyone?'

After a fulsome round of apologies from the girls, the coach driver agreed to proceed with the journey.

'They do this every time,' David whispered to Rosie. 'You'll get used to it.'

'It would be so great to stop for chips, though,' Arabella persisted. 'We've never done that before on a school trip, despite asking many times.'

'How can you stop for chips?' Sister Anne asked.

'I believe there are shops that sell chips,' Sister Anthony explained, 'though I am surprised they would be open at this time of night.'

'Have you never had chips from a chip shop? With salt and vinegar?' Rosie asked.

Sisters Anne and Anthony shook

their heads and Reverend Mother stood up and made an important announcement.

'We will be stopping for chips,' she said. 'Sister Francis gave me some money for the trip in case we needed anything and Sister Anne and Sister Anthony who have never had chips from a shop.

'Drive on, please — to the nearest chip shop. Make it one that has both salt and vinegar.'

* * *

Once back at school, even though it was well after lights out, girls ran from room to room spreading the news about stopping for chips. Very soon the entire school was talking of nothing else.

'No doubt the next music trip will be even more popular,' David said to Rosie as the coach driver pulled away down the drive, moping his face with his handkerchief, happy to have finished his evening's work at last. 'Would you like a lift home, Rosie?'

'No, it's all right, thanks, I've got my bicycle in the shed,' Rosie replied.

'Leave it there,' David suggested. 'It's very late. Tell you what, I'll give you a lift home and I can pick you up in the morning and drop you off at school.'

'Well, that's so kind but I don't want to put you out.'

'It's no bother. I have to be up early and a small detour to pick you up is of no consequence.'

'How do you know it's only a small detour?' Rosie teased. 'You don't even know where I live.'

'True,' David admitted, 'but it can't be far as you travel by bicycle.'

'Well, if you're sure, thank you.' Rosie smiled up at David. 'I accept.'

Sister Anne watched from the shadows with a large smile on her face. She couldn't wait to share what she had heard with the other nuns.

Rosie's heart beat a little faster as David drove her home. It wasn't because he was driving too fast, in fact he seemed to be driving extra slowly, maybe to prolong the journey.

No, her heart was beating faster because she was alone at night with the man of her dreams.

Pull yourself together, Rosie thought to herself. Try to remember every second — it could be the beginning of something special.

'What's it like, then, this place of yours?' David asked.

'It's a lovely room in a family house. Mr and Mrs Field had a top room they weren't using and were looking for a lodger.'

'Sounds ideal. Which way here?'

'Left turn — not this one, the next. That's it. Second house on the other side of the road.'

'Very nice,' David said, hopping out and opening the car door for Rosie. 'This way, madam,' he said, with a flourish of his hand.

Rosie giggled.

'Thank you, kind sir,' she said.

'I'll be back tomorrow morning at,

what shall we say, ten to eight?'

'Perfect.' Rosie stepped out of the car.

'Until tomorrow then,' David said.

'Thank you so much. Until tomorrow, then.'

David put his hand on Rosie's shoulder and leaned forward to give her a friendly peck on the cheek.

As he did so, Rosie turned towards him and the peck on the cheek turned into a full kiss on the mouth, much to the amazement of both parties.

Two pairs of eyes locked together for a few seconds before the kiss was repeated, this time intentionally and passionately.

'Sorry,' David said, breaking away. 'I shouldn't have done that. It's . . . it's not fair on you. I . . . I don't want anything like that.'

Rosie felt alarmed as she saw the rejection in David's face. What was wrong?

'No harm done,' she said quickly, then fled across the street and into the

Fields' house as her hopes shattered around her like a broken mirror.

Once she had got safely inside, she heard the low growl of David's car as he took off down the street.

Rosie took her shoes off so as not to wake the sleeping household and made her way up to her room in the attic, unchecked tears of disappointment streaming down her face.

Had she sent him the wrong signals? How could she face him again?

After suffering a sleepless night, Rosie got up early and prepared herself for work.

He won't give me a lift this morning, I bet, she said to herself as she trudged down the stairs. Not after the embarrassment of that kiss last night. I'd better try and get a bus to the end of the school drive then walk the rest.

As Rosie made her way to the bus stop, she heard a car horn beeping lightly. She had misjudged David. True to his word, he had turned up to give her a lift.

'What are you doing walking to the bus stop?' he demanded as he pulled up alongside the kerb.

'I thought,' Rosie began, 'under the circumstances, maybe . . . '

'What? Oh, that,' David said cheerfully. 'We're both adults, aren't we? Nothing to be bothered about. A harmless kiss that meant nothing at all.

'Glad you're not the sort of girl who takes any of that romantic nonsense seriously. No more to be said on the subject. Jump in, then.'

Rosie turned her face to the side as she sat next to David so he wouldn't see her expression.

Harmless kiss indeed, she thought to herself. Romantic nonsense?

Pulling herself together, she decided to lock David's comments away until such time as she could consider them properly. She needed to be able to face the day ahead at work without dwelling on her crushed dreams.

David switched his car radio on and the peculiarly machine-like sound of a harpsichord filled the car with intricate clattering and scratching sounds.

'Love this sort of music,' David said. 'You know where you are with this.'

Rosie decided not to say she preferred something a bit more soulful and expressive. Instead she settled for a neutral, perhaps even rather boring, topic of conversation.

'What do you think of the new syllabus for piano exams?' she asked.

With both David and Rosie firmly on a safe subject, they chatted about the merits of various pieces and their suitability for different pupils, right up to the point when they arrived at the front stretch of drive by the main door of the school.

'Mr Hart!' a girl screamed out of a top window, very soon being joined by a few friends.

'It gets wearisome, all this adulation,' David said, sweeping his hair to one side in an exaggerated theatrical gesture. 'One finds it hard to cope.'

'It seems the only virtue you don't

possess is modesty,' Rosie said as she pulled on the door handle.

'Only joking.' David laughed.

'So was I.' Rosie glared at David as she got out, then slammed the car door and made her way to the front entrance without looking back.

Let him make what he wants of that, she thought. I'm not sure I care much any more for Mr David Hart and his foolishness.

Complications

'How are the preparations going for the music festival?' Miss Spiker asked as she sat next to Rosie in the staff room.

'Very well, thank you,' Rosie answered. 'The choir know all their words from memory now and I can nearly play the accompaniments too, which helps.'

'You are a fine pianist,' Miss Spiker said, 'and of course there is no doubt Mr Hart is a great conductor. The girls don't know how lucky they are to have you two.'

Rosie smiled as she remembered how Miss Spiker had treated her when she had first arrived at Shaston. Now she seemed one of her biggest fans.

'Hello, Miss Spiker,' a bright chirpy voice said. 'How are you?'

'Why hello, Grace,' Miss Spiker

replied. 'What a pleasant surprise! I thought you would be away for longer.'

'I flew back yesterday morning,' Grace said, 'and I'm ready to get back to work.'

'You don't know Grace, do you?' Miss Spiker said to Rosie. 'Grace, meet Rosie Peach. Rosie, this is Grace Browning. I have a feeling you two young things will get on like a house on fire.'

'Lovely to meet you,' Grace said, extending a hand to Rosie. 'I've been abroad for some months now, looking after my mother. She hasn't been at all well and Reverend Mother was kind enough to give me an extended leave of absence to nurse her.'

'How is she doing?' Miss Spiker asked gently.

'I'm very pleased to report she's well on the road to recovery and my dad is adamant he can cope with looking after her on his own now.' Grace smiled.

'So here I am, looking forward to

getting back to teaching, happy in the knowledge Mum is getting better every day.'

'What do you teach?' Rosie asked.

'Children,' Grace said with a peal of laughter. 'Sorry — old joke, I know. I teach English and help out with drama too.'

'Understatement, Grace dear, a complete understatement,' Miss Spiker said. 'Rosie, I'll have you know Grace organises all the school plays plus the drama competition, not to mention preparing material for assemblies, festivals and the like, then there's the annual staff review — she always writes an amazingly funny sketch for that.'

'Steady on,' Grace said. 'You'll have me blushing! Anyway, I'd much rather hear about you, Rosie. What's your subject?'

'I teach the piano and play for the choirs,' Rosie said.

'And I'm hoping you'll be playing for the music exams this term as well, if that's all right?' Miss Spiker said. 'I suggested to Sister Francis only yesterday that you might like to do the accompanying this term. I usually do it, but it's time to hand over the reins to someone younger.'

'Of course,' Rosie said, 'no problem. Thank you for the opportunity.'

'Wonderful,' Miss Spiker said, clapping her hands. 'I'll toddle off and get you all the music you need to look at.'

'And we could have a quick cuppa,' Grace suggested to Rosie. 'I'm relying on you to fill me in on all the gossip.'

'I don't know any gossip,' Rosie said. 'Not been here long enough.'

'What about your colleague in the music department, David Hart?' Grace asked. 'Anything new there? The nuns are usually trying to marry him off to someone or other.'

'No idea,' Rosie said, trying to assume a disinterested expression.

'I've got a really soft spot for that man,' Grace confided. 'Known him for years and years. I was at school with his sister, here at Shaston. We're both old girls of the school.'

'Gosh,' Rosie said, 'how amazing.'

'His sister Isobel was a day girl, living locally, while I was one of the many who lived abroad. Sister Anthony used to take us up to Waterloo Station on the train at the end of every term and then we made our way to Heathrow and flew home for the holidays, in my case to Rome, but other girls lived all over the place — Germany, Athens, Spain, even Hong Kong. You name it, a Shaston girl lived there.'

'Another world,' Rosie said, thinking of her own childhood spent all in one place, so tame in comparison with these well-travelled girls.

'And of course we were all in love with David Hart,' Grace continued, 'especially Donna. Sometimes his sister Isobel used to invite us to their home and we were thrilled if we saw David. We thought he was terribly good-looking.'

Rosie wondered whether Grace was still in love with David. She couldn't blame her if she was because he was rather wonderful. She sighed and bit her lip.

'Time for me to go,' Grace said. 'I'm supposed to be in the sixth form centre now, covering a lesson for an absent history teacher. See you around, Rosie.'

'I look forward to it.' Rosie smiled and tried to pretend to herself that she didn't mind who else might be interested in David Hart. All of a sudden she realised the significance of what Grace had said.

'We were all in love with David Hart, especially Donna.'

Surely this Donna must be the Donna David mentioned to her at the end of the concert in Salisbury Cathedral. Donna, his late wife.

Rosie reminded herself yet again that she didn't care at all about David Hart. Gathering her things together with shaking hands, she hastened towards the door.

'Steady!' David said. 'Where are you

going in such a hurry? Nearly knocked me over. Here, let me help you pick up your music.'

'I've been chatting to Grace,' Rosie said, her face scarlet with confusion.

'Grace? She said she'd be back soon when she rang last week,' David said. 'I can't wait to see her. Do you know which way she went?'

'She's in the sixth form centre,' Rosie replied, then made her way to the music block as quickly as she could and whizzed up and down the piano playing scales at a scorching pace followed by a series of loud crashing chords until her arms ached.

'Can't wait to see Grace indeed,' she muttered to herself. 'She's welcome to him. See if I give a hoot.'

After a while, Rosie calmed down and decided to have a look at the choir accompaniments. She could manage most of them, but part of one of the pieces was proving annoyingly tricky so she played it through at the speed of a funeral lament several times before nimbly dashing her way through the tangle of notes at top speed.

'Miss Peach! Miss Peach!'

Rosie turned round and saw Arabella, Lucy and Sophia peeping round the music room door.

'You can play so fast!' Arabella said admiringly.

'Have you got time to come and see what we've found?' Sophia asked.

'In the undercroft, beneath the hall,' Lucy added. 'You'll never guess.'

'I'm not teaching for a bit,' Rosie said. 'What is it you want to show me and more importantly, why aren't you all in lessons?'

'Our teacher's away,' Arabella explained.

'Yes, Miss Boleyn, our history teacher,' Sophia said.

'Got a painful neck or something,' Lucy said, 'so we're doing research for a double lesson. Miss Browning is covering the lesson. We have to go back to the sixth form centre soon and report on what we have discovered.'

'It's such fun! We got covered in dirt

and cobwebs,' Arabella said with a giggle.

'So I see,' Rosie said. 'What are you actually studying?'

'Oh, didn't we say? The Second World War. Shaston School was used as a rest home for American bomber crews stationed in England in between missions.'

'How interesting,' Rosie said.

'We've found actual evidence we can include in our essays, down in the undercroft,' Lucy explained. 'Come and have a look.'

Rosie followed after the three madcap girls, keen to see what they had discovered.

'This is the entrance,' Sophia said as they reached a narrow stone staircase immediately outside the school's magnificent hall. 'We'll have to make our way in single file. It's a good thing none of us are too large, isn't it?'

'We decided to look in the undercroft,' Arabella said, 'because Sister Anne told us she thought the American servicemen used to spend time down here smoking and playing cards, that sort of thing. She's a fount of knowledge.'

'There didn't seem much evidence when we first looked,' Sophia said, 'but then we dragged this old cupboard to one side and discovered some writing.'

On the yellowing wall, Rosie saw scratched and faded graffiti.

Hank Marblestein was here, 1940.

'Poor bloke, saddled with a name like that!' Arabella exclaimed.

'Obviously one of the American servicemen stationed here in the War,' Lucy said.

'Look here.' Sophia pointed at some writing. 'Another piece of evidence.'

Hank loves Brenda.

All three sixth formers began laughing uncontrollably.

'Girls! Are you there?' Grace's voice echoed down the stone stairs.

'I think maybe it's time to come back to the sixth form centre and share your research,' Grace said as she appeared in the undercroft. 'My word, it's dusty. I haven't been down here since I was at school. What have you found? Hello, Rosie! Didn't expect to see you here.'

'They were so excited about their findings that they asked me to come and take a look,' Rosie explained. 'See for yourself; interesting, isn't it?'

'Certainly is,' Grace said. 'Maybe we should put on a show about the War, complete with jiving and the Lindy Hop. I'll do the drama side and you can organise the music.'

'Steady on.' Rosie laughed. 'I seem to have quite enough to do at the moment with the music festival, then there are the Christmas preparations for the choir on top of all the usual piano teaching and playing for the music exams . . . '

'Sorry,' Grace said. 'Always getting a bit carried away, that's me. Come on then, girls, time to go back.'

The three sixth formers dutifully trooped to the stairs followed by Grace and Rosie.

'When I was a girl at school here,' Grace whispered to Rosie on the staircase, 'we used to write stuff on the walls, too.'

Once Grace had hurried back to class with the sixth formers, Rosie visited the undercroft again.

'I wonder . . . ' she murmured, scanning the wartime graffiti and noticing a more modern addition the girls had missed.

Kneeling down to get a better look at some tiny writing inside a love heart at the bottom of a wall, Rosie screwed up her eyes and could just about make out:

Donna loves David H and so does Grace xxx

Blast from the Past

The following week, Rosie, David and the choir piled into a large coach and set off to Bath for the choral festival they had worked so hard for.

'Budge up!' Arabella squealed. 'You little Lower Fours need to pipe down, sit down and move up . . . Yes, I can tell you that, actually, because I'm head girl and of course it makes sense. Don't be so cheeky.'

'Everything all right?' David asked.

'Fine thanks, sir,' she replied, 'just keeping the rabble in order.'

'Will there be chips on the way back to school after the festival?' a voice cried out.

'Chips! Chips! Chips!' the chorus began.

'I'm not sure Reverend Mother did us a favour stopping for a post-concert snack after our trip to Salisbury,' David said with a groan.

'Every girl in the school seems to have heard the chip story,' Rosie said.

'Chipgate, that's what it is.'

David laughed.

'I like your sense of humour, Rosie. Now, do you mind if we have a quick look at the music? The bit after the second verse, here,' he said, pointing at the score of one of the songs the choir were due to sing that afternoon. 'I've decided to beat that section in two. I think it'll be clearer.'

'Good idea,' Rosie said, pencilling the change into her music. 'I'll be watching you like a hawk.'

'I expect you'll be looking forward to seeing the adjudicator, this Tristan bloke, again, won't you?' David continued. 'You said you were friends at college.'

'Sort of,' Rosie said, then turned to stare out of the window. 'Oh look,' she said. 'We're coming into the city. I love this view.'

'Your home city,' David said. 'I must

say, it's quite stunning, seeing the Bath stone almost golden in the sun. Where do your parents live?'

'Not in the Georgian part of the city,' Rosie said. 'The other side of the river, the Victorian bit, the not so fashionable part. What about you? Have you always lived in Dorset?'

'Yes, always. My family still live there, too — that's my sister and her husband, with Clementine, of course, and my mother lives nearby. She was widowed a few years ago. How's Clemmie getting on? She sounded really good last time I heard her play.'

'Really well,' Rosie replied. 'She's a pleasure to teach. Oh, we're here!'

The coach from Shaston was soon caught up in a queue of coaches full of eager choristers and the girls struck up a chorus of 'Why are we waiting?' much to Rosie and David's amusement.

'I suppose I should tell them to quieten down,' David said as he got to his feet.

'No need, sir,' Arabella said as she

flew down the coach, her skirt riding up and with a full face of make-up.

'Belt up, you lot!' she bawled. 'You don't want anyone thinking we're not young ladies, do you?'

'Perish the thought,' David said. 'That would never do.'

'I've got a packet of make-up wipes that might come in handy,' Rosie whispered. 'I'll stand at the bottom of the steps and dish them out to some of the girls as they leave the coach.'

Once on the pavement, Rosie saw Tristan Proudfoot making his way into the Guildhall where the festival was due to take place.

'Rosie!' he shouted. 'Lovely to see you! Someone told me you had a job at Shaston and I was wondering if you might turn up with a choir today.'

'Everything all right?' David asked as he joined Rosie. 'I say, was that the adjudicator? Striking, isn't he? Young, too.'

'Only a few months younger than me,' Rosie said with a smile.

She watched Tristan striding off, his mass of dark curls bobbing up and down in the winter sunshine and his long tailored coat flowing behind him. He looked like a young Lord Byron.

The girls had a thoroughly entertaining day listening to the other choirs and performing their own impeccable programme. Even the walking on and off went perfectly, with Arabella, Lucy and Sophia helping to keep an iron grip on the behaviour.

'I don't think that performance could have gone better,' David enthused as he sat down beside Rosie in the audience again after their performance. 'I felt you were with me every step of the way, for every note of the music. Thank you. We make a great team, don't we?'

'I felt it, too,' Rosie said. 'Oh look — Tristan is getting to his feet. He must have chosen a winner.'

'He doesn't waste much time,' David commented.

Tristan Proudfoot awarded first place to an amazing choir from Bristol.

' . . . because they bowled me over with their sensational performance . . . and I would like to award second place to Shaston Convent School. I have to praise the extremely talented accompanist from Shaston. The success of this choir is due in no small measure to her skilful piano playing. She supported and enhanced every note the choir sang.'

As Tristan looked directly at Rosie and the girls from Shaston, the choir let out a collective sigh.

'How romantic,' Arabella whispered.

'He's gorgeous,' Lucy stuttered.

'I saw him first,' Sophia said.

'He seems quite a fan of yours,' David whispered in Rosie's ear, 'though I have to say I agree with every word he said. You made the performance.'

* * *

For once the girls were quiet on the journey home, with no requests for chips or loud renditions of 'Ten Green

Bottles' or 'I've got a song that'll get on your nerves' to disturb the peace.

Rosie was lulled into a gentle sleep by the rhythm of the wheels and her head moved softly to rest on David's shoulder as she slumbered. He gazed at her oval face framed by her unruly hair and gave a deep sigh.

Could she be fond of Tristan, David wondered. He seemed pretty keen on her.

David pursed his lips and felt a pang of jealousy. Rosie was such a lovely girl. He can see straight away Tristan wasn't right for her — too arrogant by half, in David's opinion.

Relaxing back into his seat, David smiled as a future floated into his mind starring Rosie and himself, making a life together, growing old side by side . . . No, he thought angrily. I can't start anything, I really can't, not after Donna.

He felt a pang as he remembered the kiss he had shared with Rosie. He wondered if he had hurt Rosie's feelings the other day when he said the kiss meant nothing.

But it was for the best, he thought.

* * *

Reverend Mother was waiting for the coach to return and was thrilled to hear the exciting news of the choir's triumph.

'Well done, girls, and well done Mr Hart and Miss Peach. We're all so proud of you.'

As the girls came off the coach, more and more nuns assembled to congratulate them.

'Straight to tea, girls,' Sister Francis commanded. 'And yes, Sophia, there are cakes.'

'I can't believe I fell asleep on the way back,' Rosie said, embarrassed.

'Don't worry,' David replied. 'You didn't snore — not much, anyway.'

Rosie laughed as she set off to get her bike to cycle home to Shaston. She still felt half asleep as she pedalled her way down the drive. It seemed a real effort to move her legs.

Silly me, she thought, I'm in the wrong gear. I'll slow down then change . . .

Rosie wobbled on her bicycle as she attempted to co-ordinate hand and foot to change gear, then pressed the brake by mistake and somehow tumbled on to the ground. She lay there for a few seconds to catch her breath, then moved gently.

Good, she thought. A few bruises, that's all.

'Rosie!' David's car screeched to a halt a few yards away and he ran towards her, agitated beyond belief.

'Rosie! Are you all right? Don't move. I can run back and call an ambulance. You mustn't move. How's your neck? You need to protect your neck.'

David knelt over her and stroked her hand tenderly.

'I couldn't bear it if anything happened to you.'

Rosie looked at him in wonder, and he suddenly recollected himself.

'It . . . it was the shock,' David said. 'I'm not good with accidents. You're sure you're all right?'

'Absolutely fine,' Rosie said, jumping up. 'See? No bones broken. My tights are laddered and that's about it.'

David looked at the ladder in Rosie's tights then looked away quickly, all of a sudden feeling flustered.

'I could give you a lift?' he offered.

'No, thanks. I need to get my bike home and your car's far too small to fit it in the back,' Rosie said firmly. 'Honestly, David, I'm fine.'

After Rosie had insisted several more times she felt fit and well, David finally said he was happy for her to continue her journey home. He drove slowly behind her all the way down the drive to make sure, though, waving goodbye as they reached the main road.

Christmas is on its Way

The smell of fresh pine mingled with the ever-present fragrance of highly polished wood, filling the vast entrance hall and floating up the broad wide staircase.

Crowds of girls perched on every step and sat squashed together on the floor surrounding the enormous Christmas tree at the foot of the stairs. The entire school was assembled for the annual festive carols the night before the end of term, with the school choir leading the unaccompanied singing.

'Silent Night . . . ' they all sang and a tingle ran down Rosie's spine. So simple and yet so beautiful.

She felt a contentment sweeping over her, swiftly followed by exhaustion. It had been a whirlwind term, full of activity and music, but Rosie was glad it was coming to an end for a couple of weeks as she really didn't think she could face many more early mornings.

'You get used to it,' her friend Grace had said that morning as she had noticed Rosie yawning in assembly. 'The first term is the worst. After a while you learn to pace yourself.'

Rosie thought back to all she been involved in that term — the trip to Salisbury, the music festival, all those piano lessons, several carol services in the chapel she had somehow been roped in to help with, the big Christmas Concert, playing for the music exams . . . the list was endless.

Miss Spiker seemed to be taking more and more of a back seat and increasingly relied on Rosie to help out.

'Now we turn to our next carol,' Reverend Mother's strong voice rang out. ''Away in a Manger' . . . '

Rosie noticed David's eyes suddenly filled with tears as the girls started singing. What a big softie he is, she thought affectionately.

'The stars in the bright sky . . . ' Sister Anne and Sister Anthony quavered, sitting side by side with peaceful expressions.

They've always had Christmas together, Rosie thought. That's amazing. They must know each other inside out.

'And to end with,' Sister Francis said, ' 'Hark the Herald'.'

The girls jumped to their feet for the last rousing song, thinking no doubt of the fun they would have in the holidays, back in their own homes with their families. Massive cheering broke out at the end, led by Arabella, Lucy and Sophia.

'Quieten down, girls,' Reverend Mother said, 'if you can. Those of you who are travelling to Waterloo tomorrow on the train with Sister Anthony, I hope you have an uneventful journey back to your families abroad and to everyone, I wish you all a very special and happy Christmas break.'

'Happy Christmas!' Sister Francis

shouted over the din. 'You are dismissed! Staff, please follow us to the blue parlour where refreshments are available.'

'We get an annual glass of sherry,' Grace whispered in Rosie's ear as they made their way through the throng to the parlour, 'with some delicious home-made nibbles. The cheese straws are incredible.'

'Excellent news,' Rosie said. 'Can't wait.'

'Grace, let me pass you a glass of sherry,' David offered. 'Here you are. And one for you, too, Rosie?'

'Thank you,' Rosie said, suddenly wondering about the graffiti she had seen in the undercroft again, about both Donna and Grace loving David. She hadn't mentioned this to Grace yet, hadn't liked to, but her curiosity was bubbling up nevertheless.

David did seem very friendly with Grace but then they had known each other a long time and Grace had been a friend to both his sister and his wife.

'So, a good term?' David asked. 'Hope we haven't put you off teaching.'

'I've loved it,' Rosie said. 'The girls are so lively and curious, they make every lesson fun and the surroundings are like a dream. I still can't believe I'm working in such a beautiful environment as Shaston. Every day I cycle up the drive seems magical.'

'Wait a bit longer,' Grace said with a laugh, 'and you'll feel more cynical, like the rest of us. It'll wear off, all this excitement.'

'I know you're teasing,' Rosie said. 'You love this place as much as I do, otherwise why would you be working at Shaston after spending your school days here as well?'

'Maybe I couldn't get a job anywhere else?' Grace joked.

'Well I enjoy teaching at Shaston and my sister loved being at school here,' David said, 'but then she was a day girl like Clementine. I think it can be tough for the boarders sometimes, especially when they're very young.'

'True,' Grace remarked. 'I try to forget about how wretched I was when I first arrived. My parents wanted me to have an English education. Living in Rome, this seemed a good option, but I tell you, coming from the gentle warmth of an Italian autumn to the draughty damp English climate took some getting used to when I first arrived.'

'What about your other friends?' Rosie asked, determined to bring the conversation round to the mysterious Donna. 'Did they all live abroad?'

'Some did, but many lived in other parts of the country,' Grace said as she sipped her sherry. 'One of my friends was sent here because her family lived in Blackpool and her parents didn't want her to speak with a Blackpool accent, or so she said!'

'Mmm, makes a good story, but I'm not sure that would be the main motivation for spending all that money on the fees,' David said with a laugh. 'I'm going to have a chat with Miss

Spiker now I think, so if you'll excuse me, ladies . . . '

'Where did Donna live?' Rosie asked Grace.

'Donna? You mean David's Donna? Her family lived in Devon.'

'And what was she like?' Rosie persisted.

'We were good friends when we were at school,' Grace said. 'Donna was a bit wilder than most of us, but she was always tremendous fun, a great mimic, life and soul of the party, all that.

'I do remember one occasion when she decided to climb out of the bedroom window on to the roof,' she added, 'and dance the Charleston in the middle of the night. Thank goodness we got her down before the nuns noticed.

'Anyway, once I left school I only saw her occasionally. I was away at college training to be a teacher and I spent the holidays in Rome with my parents.

'I suppose I wasn't surprised when she got engaged to David and of course I went to the wedding — what a beautiful occasion that was, down in Totnes in Devon where her childhood home was.'

Grace looked at her empty sherry glass.

'Poor Donna. She would have been twenty-five now, same age as me and, of course, David's sister, Isobel. It was such a shock when she died.'

'How did . . . Oh er, hello, David. Did you have a good chat with Miss Spiker?'

'I did,' he said. 'Now, what are you two doing in the holidays? Presume you're off to Rome shortly, Grace?'

'Yes,' Grace replied. 'I had thought of asking my parents over here for Christmas although my cottage is so tiny it would have been quite a squeeze, but on balance it's better if I go to them. My mother is much recovered but she's better off not making a long journey for the time being.'

'Very wise,' David said. 'And Rosie — are you going back to Bath?'

'Yes, I'll be back home with my

parents for the break.'

'I'm giving an organ recital in Bath,' David said, 'at the end of December, at St Stephen's. Do you know the church? It's right at the top of Lansdown.'

'Oh, yes,' Rosie answered. 'It's the one perched on the hill — you can see it from all over the city.'

'If you come and hear me, at least I'll have an audience of one,' David said with a broad grin.

Grace laughed.

'Really, David, you are impossible. You know full well the church will be packed and Rosie would be lucky to get a ticket even now. Your recitals are immensely popular.

'Besides, I'm sure Rosie has lots of friends in Bath she needs to catch up with. She doesn't want to waste her time listening to you playing the organ.'

How weird, Rosie thought. It's almost as if Grace hopes I won't see David in the holidays. Does she want him for herself?

'I'd love to come,' Rosie said, 'if there are any tickets left, of course.'

'I have a spare one in the staff room,' David said. 'I'll give it to you tomorrow.'

'Thank you.'

Not long after that, Rosie decided to go home and as she made her way to collect her bicycle, she heard footsteps behind her in the corridor.

'Rosie!' Grace called. 'Rosie! Wait for me! May I have a quick word?'

'Of course,' Rosie said. 'I'm all ears. What is it? You look worried.'

'Nothing really, it's just that . . . Oh, this is so difficult but I wanted to, well, to warn you off David.' Grace stood in front of Rosie, the dark glossy hair she had inherited from her Italian mother glowing in the light and her nut-brown eyes flashing.

'To warn me off him? What do you mean?'

'Rosie, David isn't the man you think he is. He's a very complex character. When he and Donna were together, well, let's just say it wasn't all plain sailing and that was mostly David's fault, in my humble opinion. He's a lovely man, don't get me wrong, but he can be very suspicious and jealous for no reason.

'Donna had to put up with a lot when they were married. I know I said I hardly ever saw her after we left school but we used to write to each other from time to time, particularly once she was married.'

'I don't know what to say,' Rosie began, 'except whatever makes you think I'm interested in David? He's a colleague, no more, no less.'

'I'm relieved if that's the case,' Grace said. 'I didn't want you to get taken in by him, maybe led on into a situation you can't handle. I don't think he's ready for a serious commitment and you don't strike me as the sort of girl who's only looking for a fling.'

'Thank you for informing me,' Rosie said rather stiffly.

'Oh, now I've offended you,' Grace

said, her cheeks reddening. 'I'm really sorry.'

'No offence taken,' Rosie said. 'Now if you'll excuse me, my bicycle awaits. I want to get home before the wind whips up too much.'

Grace looked after Rosie's departing figure sadly. Perhaps I shouldn't have said anything, she thought. But I can't let it happen again.

* * *

Rosie pedalled furiously, taking her anger out on her calf muscles until they throbbed. How dare Grace say anything so personal to her about David? She wasn't even interested in him anyway. Too arrogant by half and prone to kissing someone then saying it didn't mean anything.

A small rational voice inside her head pointed out that Grace was only putting into words some suspicions that Rosie herself had, but her heart took over at this point and she decided Grace must be motivated by some sort of jealousy and was trying to get David for herself by putting Rosie off.

And what is this about Donna, Rosie wondered. She seems to be considered some sort of saint. No-one is a saint in real life but people often talk of the dead in that way, she reasoned.

By the time she got home, Rosie had composed herself and decided there must be a perfectly logical explanation for what was or wasn't going on. The problem was, she didn't have all the facts yet, so she resolved to find out more about Donna.

She would start tomorrow by asking Sister Anne how she had died.

* * *

'I thought you knew the answer to that,' Sister Anne said as she stood with Rosie near the laundry and the cycle shed the next morning.

'I thought everybody knew that but I forgot you're still fairly new — it's because you've settled in so well. It seems as if you've been here for ages, doesn't it? What was it you asked again?'

'I asked about Donna, Mr Hart's wife. I asked you how she died. She was so young.'

'It was a car accident. Terrible shock, it was when we heard that one of our girls had died at the tender age of twenty-two. Her parents were inconsolable, Mr Hart, too, of course, and all her friends from school.'

Rosie gasped.

'How terrible. Was it a motorway crash?'

'The car went over a cliff. Poor Donna was killed outright.'

Rosie's eyes welled with tears.

'Don't be sad,' Sister Anne said. 'There's nothing to be done. It happened. We can't change the past, only the future.'

'Thank you for being so frank, Sister Anne,' Rosie said.

She noticed David's MG pulling into

the car park at that point and her heart went out to him. What a tragedy. No wonder he seemed a bit contradictory at times. It must take ages to get over something like that.

'He needs help to get over his loss,' Sister Anne said and she put her hand on Rosie's shoulder. 'You can help him.'

Rosie's mind went back to when she had fallen off her bicycle on the drive and David had jumped out of his car, distraught. He had said then he wasn't good with accidents. Of course, it all made sense. He was upset because he was thinking of another accident. He was thinking of Donna.

The last morning of term passed in a frenzy of tidying and high spirits. By late morning parents had started turning up in their cars to collect the girls and their gigantic trunks.

'This way,' Sister Francis shouted to the cars as she directed the traffic streaming up the drive. 'Happy Christmas to you all!'

Reverend Mother waved sedately to

the families as she stood outside the grand front entrance and Sister Anne shooed the cars back down the drive with great efficiency.

'It was like a military operation,' Rosie said to Grace as they sat over a coffee in the staff room. 'I'm seriously impressed.'

'And all the while Sister Anthony is having the time of her life on the train to Waterloo with the girls who live abroad.' Grace stirred her coffee. 'Any biscuits? I'm peckish this morning.'

'About yesterday . . . ' Rosie began tentatively, 'I'm sorry if I seemed rude and ungrateful when you tried to talk to me about David.'

'I should never have said anything,' Grace replied. 'It's none of my business.'

'I'm pleased you did,' Rosie said thoughtfully. 'Sister Anne spoke to me this morning too. I hadn't realised Donna had died in a car accident. David must feel terrible. So traumatic.'

'Yes, to be driving one minute then

over a cliff the next,' Grace said. 'It doesn't bear thinking about.'

'Let's not think about it then,' Rosie said.

'I agree,' Grace said. 'Friends?'

'Friends,' Rosie said with a grin.

'Glad you two are having fun,' David said, appearing from nowhere. 'Do you mind if I join you? I've been picking up bits of choral music from the organ loft in the chapel.

'The girls were supposed to tidy it all up after the last service this morning — Arabella and Lucy said they'd organise a team to help — but I guess they had better things to do.'

'Like throw glitter around,' Grace suggested.

'And eat mince pies,' Rosie added.

'Here's the ticket for my recital I promised you,' David said as he handed Rosie an envelope. 'Hope to see you there.'

'Thanks,' Rosie said. 'I expect you're quite busy over Christmas, playing for services and so on.'

'Yes, I am,' David said. 'I'm finishing

off by playing for Midnight Mass in my local village church, then I'm going to my sister's family for Christmas Day. It's always a riot with little Clemmie around. My mother will be coming over for the day, too.'

'Do you have an Italian Christmas or an English one out in Rome, Grace?' Rosie asked.

'Bit of both,' Grace answered. 'My dad would be heartbroken not to have his turkey and stuffing and Mum cooks all the traditional Italian food as well. We don't go hungry!

'My brothers pitch up with their wives and children for lunch, then tons of friends drop in during the afternoon. It's quite a madhouse.'

'Sounds hectic,' Rosie said. 'It's only me at home with my parents. Quiet, but lovely — perfect.'

A bit like you, David thought as he sat beside Rosie. He realised he was falling in love with her and felt both joy and fear in equal measure.

The staff room started to empty as

the teachers hastened off to their classrooms to collect their belongings before making their way home for the holidays.

Reverend Mother had emphasised the need to remove all personal belongings not only for pupils but for staff, too, as during the Christmas break the nuns were planning to embark on an intensive programme of domestic cleaning.

'Bye, everyone!'

'Have a great Christmas.'

'And a Happy New Year!'

'See you all next term.'

Rosie made her way outside and down to the music hut behind the hall as she thought she had left her copy of Chopin nocturnes there.

'Ah, good,' she said when she discovered it sitting on the piano. 'I thought I'd left this here after Lucy's last lesson.'

As she made her way out of the room, she saw a tall figure outlined in the doorway.

'Only me,' David said. 'I've left a few books here I need to collect. Sorry, I didn't mean to startle you.'

Rosie noticed a sprig of something hanging over the doorway.

'Look what one of the girls has left,' David whispered, pointing up at the piece of mistletoe and forgetting all about his resolution not to start anything with Rosie because of Donna. 'Do you think perhaps a Christmas kiss would be in order?'

Rosie was in his arms before she could remind herself she wasn't at all interested in him and sometimes she even suspected him of not being a particularly nice or trustworthy person. Their lips locked together passionately and the two of them clung to each other like lost souls.

'Rosie,' David whispered into her hair, 'my Rosie. When you fell off your bike, I realised how fond of you I am . . . Darling Rosie.'

As chance would have it, a door banged in the distance and so they leaped apart from each other, remembering they were still at work, even if term had ended half an hour ago.

'Better go,' Rosie said.

'Yes,' David agreed. 'You'll come to my recital?'

'Wouldn't miss it,' Rosie said fervently.

Once David had found his books, they made their way together round to the front of the building and set off, David to his car and Rosie to her bicycle, allowing themselves a brief wave to each other as they parted.

Sister Anne watched them affectionately from an upstairs window and hoped her efforts with the mistletoe had hurried things along. She had confiscated the sprig only that morning when she found Arabella trying to tie it on to the wing mirror of a teacher's car.

Sister Anne had decided the mistletoe would be much more useful hanging up in the music department.

'If music be the food of love, play on,' she whispered.

Home for Christmas

Rosie opened the envelope David had given her with the ticket for his recital as soon as she got back to the Fields' house that evening. How kind, she thought. Not only has he given me a ticket, but there's a lovely Christmas card as well.

She held the picture of a glittery snow-covered church up to the light so that she could make it sparkle even more.

Inside David had written:

'Hope to see you at the recital. Maybe come and say hello afterwards? D'

Rosie felt a little disappointed there were no kisses after the abrupt 'D'. She wasn't to know David had sat agonising for ages, pen poised, trying to decide whether or not to put in kisses.

A thousand kisses wouldn't even be

enough, his heart had told him, while his head had reminded him that he had said he didn't want any romance in his life. Remember what happened last time.

* * *

Rosie woke early the next day in a buoyant mood and decided to pop out to the shops in Shaston as she had a few last minute odds and ends to get before she travelled back to Bath. She was knitting her parents a stocking. Having not been able to think what to give them for Christmas, Grace had suggested to Rosie she filled a stocking with their favourite treats.

'It was something I did last year,' Grace said, 'for a certain someone I was keen on.'

'Who was that?'

'Not worth saying,' Grace had answered with a quick cough, 'because it didn't work out. Although it might this year. Who knows? I always have hope! It's someone I've known for a long time, since childhood in fact.'

Rosie frowned as she remembered this exchange. Could Grace have been referring to David? Oh, why was life so complicated?

Hastening along the streets to the local department store, Hine and Parsons, Rosie found it was still closed.

Oh dear, she thought, there's only one thing for it. I need to have a hot drink and maybe even a sticky bun in the tea room opposite while I wait for Hine and Parsons to open.

Seating herself at a cosy table at the back, Rosie busied herself writing a list of treats she could buy to fill her parents' stocking.

Ten minutes later she'd finished her list and her snack, and set off on her errands again.

Before she got up from the table, she noticed two familiar figures outside the window — David and Grace. They appeared to be arguing.

I won't go out now, Rosie thought. I

don't want them to see me.

Within a few minutes, Grace had walked in one direction and David in the other.

Grace said she was flying out to Rome today, Rosie remembered, so what is she still doing here?

I suppose her flight could be in the afternoon, she reasoned, and she has every right to be here as Shaston is the nearest town to the village she lives in, but why meet up with David? Was it a chance meeting or did they arrange to meet?

Rosie waited until she was sure the coast was completely clear and then scuttled off to complete her errands, but the joy she had felt upon waking that morning had dissipated and she felt unsure of herself again.

* * *

Meanwhile, David had made his way back to his cottage at top speed in his sports car.

How dare Grace talk to me like that, he fumed silently. I've a good mind to tell her the truth.

David had bumped into Grace by chance when out trying to start his Christmas shopping. His sister Isobel had given him a list of suggestions for the family as he always found choosing presents tricky, but after his encounter with Grace, David decided to abandon his shopping trip and try again another day.

He had so much music to organise for various Christmas services that he thought he would be better off doing that. It might help him simmer down.

* * *

'We've missed you,' Rosie's mother Sheila said later as she welcomed her daughter back home. 'We haven't done the tree yet. We waited as we thought you'd like us to decorate it all together as we usually do.'

Rosie's eyes shone with happiness as

she embraced her. She was overjoyed to be home.

'I like what you've done with your hair,' Sheila said. 'It looks really pretty swept up like that.'

'Thank you,' Rosie said with a smile. 'It's so good to be home.'

'Quite a few Christmas cards have arrived for you,' Brian said. 'I've put them in your room.'

'Thanks, Dad, I'll open them later,' Rosie replied. 'Now, what about this tree? Shall we get started?'

Rosie spent a magical time with her parents dressing the tree with all the favourite decorations and ornaments she remembered from her childhood and when they had finished, she stepped back and surveyed their handiwork. Christmas had started at last!

Unpacking in her bedroom later, she noticed the pile of cards her father had mentioned.

There were a couple from old school friends and a larger amount from her college friends, now dispersed all over the country, mostly teaching music as she was.

Surely not, Rosie thought as she held up a large envelope with instantly recognisable flamboyant writing.

Surely Tristan hasn't sent me anything? I thought he'd got the message when we were at college.

Tearing open the envelope, Rosie found herself looking at a brightly coloured cartoon-like card with a picture of Father Christmas surrounded by rather scantily clad elves. Inside Tristan had written:

'So FAB to see you, darling Rosie, at the festival recently. Have the best Christmas ever, with oodles of love, your own Tristan.'

Fab? Oodles of love? Rosie groaned. When they had been at college he had had so many girlfriends everyone had lost count, but he was always intrigued by the ones who didn't seem to fall for him — these he regarded as a special challenge.

Rosie fell into this category and no

matter how many times she had explained to him that she only wanted to be friends, he didn't get it and continued to pester her.

'Shame,' Rosie whispered to the card, 'because I liked you as a friend. You're a great musician and we were in some fab' concerts together.'

She put the card down with a smile and continued unpacking her suitcase, pulling out the nearly completed stocking and the tiny wrapped presents ready to be packed inside for her parents.

* * *

In Rome, Grace was helping out with the family Christmas preparations, overjoyed to realise her mother was now fully recovered from her illness.

It'll be the best celebration ever, she thought, especially if he rings.

'Roberto was asking after you,' Grace's mother said as they were chopping herbs and garlic in the kitchen together. 'He rang to ask when you would back.'

'Really?' Grace's face bloomed with happiness.

'Yes, really. I asked him to pop over this afternoon. Hope you don't mind.'

'What time? Does my hair look all right? Perhaps I should change my clothes?' Grace pulled frantically at the apron she was wearing over her shirt and jeans.

'So you do like him?' Grace's mother said as she laughed and hugged her daughter.

Grace had known Roberto for what seemed like for ever. He was the son of friends of her parents and a good friend of one of her brothers, too.

She had grown very fond of him over the years but had always suspected he thought of her as a sort of sister.

However, last summer and early autumn, when she had been staying longer in Rome to look after her mother during her illness, Roberto had often come to the house and offered his help and support.

Grace hadn't told anyone of their budding romance. It was such early days and she didn't want to spoil things, but now her mother had said he was coming round and suddenly she couldn't wait to see him. This was going to be a brilliant Christmas after all, Grace felt sure of it.

* * *

'Uncle David! I can see Uncle David!' Clementine jumped down from the window sill and ran towards her mother, Isobel. 'His car is out there! He's arrived at last!'

'Sorry, everyone,' David said as he managed to squeeze through the front door, laden down with presents, most of the bulky ones for Clementine. 'I slept in a little this morning.'

'You must be worn out,' his mother said as she stepped forward to give him a Christmas hug. 'We all thought you played beautifully at Midnight Mass yesterday — actually, I think I mean today, don't I?'

'Yes, earlier today. It was a lovely service,' David agreed, 'and great to see you there, Clemmie. How come you're not tired now? You were up so late.'

'It's too exciting!' Clementine screamed, then ran round the room with her arms outstretched like a demented aeroplane.

'Maybe come into the kitchen and help me for a few minutes, Clemmie?' Isobel suggested. 'A bit of quiet time?'

'Will you come too, Uncle David?' Clementine asked, slipping her hand through David's to drag him to the kitchen.

'Certainly will, if there's a strong coffee on offer,' David said. 'Lead the way.'

David's mother Valerie sat down next to Isobel's husband, Rod.

'It's so kind of you to have me to stay over the holiday,' Valerie said. 'It's really lovely for me to feel part of the family and to see little Clemmie open her presents.'

'Our Christmas wouldn't be complete without you,' Rod replied, 'and you know you are welcome any time, not only on high days and holidays.'

'So thoughtful of you,' Valerie said, her voice muffled by the handkerchief she held to her eyes. 'I'm still getting used to being on my own.'

'No tears, Mum, not on Christmas day,' David said, coming back into the sitting room with a tray of steaming mugs of coffee and mince pies. 'That's better. Dry your eyes now. What shall we do now? Any ideas?'

'Presents?' Clementine whispered, having been told by her father to keep the noise down a little.

'What's that? Did someone say something?' David asked. 'I thought I heard someone asking a question but I must have imagined it. Never mind. Shall we play cards? Monopoly?'

'Uncle David!' Clementine squealed. 'It's time for the presents. You know it is.'

'I've had a look but I don't think any

of the presents are for you,' David said solemnly.

'I've had a look, too, and I know one of them is for you, because I wrapped it up,' Clementine said. 'Here, under the tree. Please open this one first. It's from me to you.'

She handed David a large flat box covered in red and green paper, with several thick layers of Sellotape fastening each end of the parcel.

'Beautifully wrapped,' David observed. 'Shame to open it really. I think I'll put it back.'

'No!' Clementine shouted.

David shook the present gently.

'It's making a strange sort of rattling noise. Is it a snake in a box?'

'It's chocolates,' Clementine squealed. 'Oh, I forgot! I wasn't supposed to say.'

'Oh, David, do stop teasing the poor girl,' Valerie said, starting to laugh. 'You are incorrigible, exactly like your father.'

'What does incorrigibabble mean?' Clementine asked.

'Intensely annoying,' Isobel said, giggling as she flopped into an arm-chair. 'Your Uncle David's speciality. The turkey can look after itself for a while now. Time for a break.'

'Put your feet on this stool to rest, Mummy,' Clementine said, 'and then may we . . . '

'Yes,' Isobel and Rod said together. 'Present time!'

* * *

A few days after Christmas, David drove over to Bath on the morning of his organ recital. He had arranged to practise on the instrument in St Stephen's at eleven o'clock for a couple of hours, leaving the afternoon free to relax before giving the recital at seven in the evening.

'I do hope Rosie will turn up for the concert,' he thought as he drove along with the first chorus from 'Bach's Christmas Oratorio' blasting from his car cassette player.

David stopped singing as he thought back to saying 'I do,' at his wedding to Donna all those years ago in a tiny church in Truro. Who would have known the marriage would be over within the year, with Donna dying so tragically?

He thought his sister Isobel had been trying to talk to him about his situation on Christmas Day when he was helping out in the kitchen after lunch, but he hadn't wanted to have a heart to heart.

He wasn't ready for that. What was it she had said? He tried to remember. Something like:

'You can't go on blaming yourself. It wasn't your fault. You deserve some happiness again.'

David switched the music off as it was beginning to irritate him.

'Perhaps Isobel understands,' he whispered. 'If anyone does, it will be her.'

* * *

While David was practising the organ in St Stephen's, Rosie was in Bath having a look around the sales with her mother.

Rosie's father Brian had arranged to pick them up by car as he knew from experience how heavily laden they would be with bargains.

'There's your father!' Sheila exclaimed. 'It's so kind of him to come and pick us up.'

'I see you have saved even more money than usual this year in the sales,' Brian said as he staggered to the car, insisting on carrying all the bags by himself.

'We had a great time, didn't we, Rosie?' Sheila said. 'Now, home, Jeeves, if you please.'

'I think I might walk home,' Rosie said. 'Gosh, it feels good to have got rid of those bags. I might take a wander round the Circus and go on up to Lansdown first. I've really missed Bath.'

'If you're sure,' Sheila said. 'Don't be too long, the weather's turning colder.'

'Enjoy the sights,' Brian added.

Rosie strode purposefully past the rows of stunning Georgian town houses, on and on, higher and higher, until she paused for breath outside St Stephen's, the church where David would be giving his recital that evening.

She felt her heart beating faster and not only because of the long climb up the hill.

What was that beautiful sound? Could David already be here practising? Rosie made her way up the steep steps and crept into a back pew. She was transfixed by the majestic sounds floating down from the organ loft.

'Bother!' David's voice said. 'F sharp! I knew that.'

After a few seconds the music continued weaving its magic and Rosie felt transported to heaven. She closed her eyes and drifted off into a light catnap. Climbing that hill exhausted me, was her last conscious thought before she felt someone shaking her shoulder.

'Rosie! It is you. I thought so. The

concert isn't until tonight, you know.'

'Hello, David,' she said. 'I was in the city and thought it would be a nice idea to pop up here. I heard music playing so came in and sat down. Before I knew it, I'd fallen asleep!'

'Hope the audience stays awake longer than you did,' David joked.

'Your playing was marvellous,' Rosie explained in confusion. 'It's a long walk up here and I felt tired . . . '

As her voice trailed away, she realised David was pulling her leg and she smiled back at him.

'I'm going to take a stroll down the hill into the city,' David said. 'Would you care to join me? Perhaps you could show me the sights? You know the place so much better than I do.'

'Love to,' Rosie said, 'but since we're already up here, let's go and see Lansdown Crescent first — it's so beautiful. Only a short walk away, I promise! And there's Somerset Place . . . '

David and Rosie slipped out of the church and spent a delightful couple of hours walking and talking, though it was doubtful whether either of them took in many of the sights, mostly having eyes only for each other.

'You'll come and see me after the recital?' David asked as he reluctantly agreed that perhaps Rosie should go home as her parents would be wondering where she had got to.

'Of course!' she cried. 'What will you do now, for the rest of the afternoon?'

'More practice,' David said with a grin. 'Then I like to sit quietly for a bit. I'm not good company just before a concert, I can tell you. No matter how experienced you are, the old nerves still kick in.'

'It's going to be fantastic,' Rosie said as she waved goodbye.

'As long as the audience don't fall asleep,' David shouted after her.

* * *

Rosie trembled with anticipation as she arrived at the church 15 minutes before the start of the recital. She was wearing a new scarlet coat her mother had given her for Christmas and underneath, one of her purchases from the morning: a gorgeous turquoise dress with an ethnic print and tiny beaded detailing.

She had managed to tame her shining hair and she was wearing almost as much eye make-up as the girls at Shaston did when they went on outings.

'You look a million dollars,' a familiar voice drawled.

'Tristan!' Rosie gasped as she spun round to see the unwelcome vision. 'What are you doing here?'

'I'm here for the recital, sweetie,' he said. 'I'm staying with an old mate for the weekend. There's quite a few London folk coming down for the concert this evening. Perhaps you don't know how well thought of David Hart is as an organist?'

'Of course I know how good David is,' Rosie said indignantly. 'I'm here for musical reasons, after all.'

'Really?' Tristan said, taking a drag from his cigarette.

'Tristan!' Rosie squeaked. 'You can't smoke here. It's a church.'

'Come outside then while I finish it off,' Tristan said as he put his arm round Rosie and bundled her towards the porch and outside on to the steps, where they collided with a very nervous looking David.

'David!' Tristan said, extending his hand. 'David Hart! Great choir performance back in the autumn. Well done. Can't wait to hear you play this evening. The second piece is an absolute favourite of mine.

'You know Rosie, of course. She's an absolute favourite of mine too. Known her for years — we go way back.'

'Taking a last bit of air,' David said, 'before I play. You know how it is.'

'Absolutely,' Tristan agreed. 'Break a leg and all that.'

'Er, thank you,' David said.

'What did you have to say that for?' Rosie asked furiously once David had gone back into the church. ' 'We go way back?' What are you implying?'

'A man's got to have hope,' Tristan said imploringly, suddenly going down on one knee and holding his hands up to Rosie in supplication. 'Give me hope!'

Rosie giggled.

'Get up,' she said. 'You're an idiot.'

Neither Tristan nor Rosie realised David had popped back to the steps for a moment as he had remembered he had left his music next to one of the pillars. He grabbed it quickly, pausing only to glance in horror at Tristan and then fled inside to get ready.

'Let me make this quite clear,' Rosie said, 'for the umpteenth time, there is no 'us'. We went to college together and we're friends — sort of — but you're not to try it on with me again. Give up. Please.'

Tristan grinned.

'So there's hope?' he asked.

'No,' Rosie said, 'because I'm in love with someone else.'

We'll see about that, sweetie, Tristan thought as he watched Rosie storming back into the church. Indeed we will.

The atmosphere in the concert was electric. Never had David played so fast and furiously, nor so tenderly, sadly and sweetly. He played as if his life depended on it, with every dramatic possibility in the music taken full advantage of.

When the fortissimo chords at the end of the last piece had sounded, the entire audience sat on the edges of their seats, spellbound, no-one daring to be the first to applaud, then shouts of 'Bravo, bravo!' filled the church and the audience rose as one, with wild clapping and cheering that could be heard by passers-by on the pavements outside.

Rosie felt so proud of David as he came down to take a bow in the main body of the church. Making her way towards him through the throng, she saw Tristan was already talking to David, whispering something in his ear.

Everyone was crowding round David now, holding their programmes out for him to autograph and then at last Rosie managed to stand before David, her David.

'I loved it,' she said. 'Beautiful! Well done.'

'Thanks,' David snapped. 'See you at school next term, no doubt,' he added, before turning on his heel to sign another programme.

As Rosie ran from the church, soft snowflakes fell on to her head and tears threatened to flow down her cheeks. Not now, she thought. Let me get away first before I give in to my feelings. Oh, what on earth has gone wrong?

David came to his senses almost immediately and realised how rude he had been to Rosie.

Why should I believe what Tristan has just told me, he asked himself angrily. I won't believe it unless I hear it from Rosie's own lips. Where is she? I hope I'm not too late to catch her.

Slipping and sliding down the icy

pavements at the side of the church, with the snow starting to fall more heavily now, Rosie thought she heard someone calling her name.

'Rosie! Want a lift, Rosie?' Tristan shouted from his car as he drove up beside her. 'Your parents still live up on the hill on the other side of the city, don't they? Beechen Cliff?'

'That's right,' Rosie sobbed. 'Do you know, I'd really appreciate a lift. I want to get home quickly. If you wouldn't mind?'

'Stay there while I open the door for you,' Tristan commanded.

David howled in anguish as he stood on the steps of St Stephen's. Through the swirling snow he could make out Tristan's distinctive tall figure and Rosie in her scarlet coat, getting into Tristan's car.

Cold and Frosty

'There's ice on the windows!' Arabella shivered as she tied a piece of string around a Mars Bar.

'Yes, and it's on the inside!' Lucy shrieked as she ran her hands down the window and collected ice chips under her fingernails. 'I sincerely hope Sophia appreciates what we're doing for her.'

Arabella and Lucy were engaged in the delicate art of getting much needed sugar supplies to their friend Sophia, who was tucked up in bed in the infirmary below a dormitory in Slum Alley.

The two conspirators had slipped away from an unsupervised library lesson to put their plan into action, namely to lower a Mars Bar out of the window of the dormitory and deliver it to the invalid in the room beneath.

Finally managing to fix the string to

the chocolate bar, Arabella flung open the casement window and the treat began its tricky descent to the infirmary window below.

Sophia was roused from her sleep by a tapping sound on the window pane next to her bed. She had been languishing there for a couple of days with a fever and sore throat. The nuns believed in isolating ill pupils, always terrified of a recurrence of the legendary flu epidemics of earlier times, and thus Sophia was not only feeling rough but also extremely bored.

'What . . . ?' she said in amazement. 'Has my temperature gone up again? That looks like a Mars Bar on a string! Better than a 'Puppet on a String', I suppose.'

'Sophia! Sophia! Open up.' Arabella leaned out of the dormitory window a little further while she swung the string backwards and forwards, tapping quite aggressively on the pane below.

Sophia's face split into a radiant smile as she shuffled out of bed and opened the window.

'Good old Arabella and Lucy,' she cried. 'I knew they wouldn't forget me!'

Sophia managed to grab the chocolate as it swung past, stuffing it hastily into her dressing-gown pocket.

'Thanks a million,' she yelled, before she closed the window.

'I'll have that, if you don't mind,' a stern voice said.

Sophia looked round and saw Reverend Mother standing there, trying hard to keep a straight face.

'That is no way to behave, young lady,' Reverend Mother continued, 'shouting like a fishwife out of the window. Arabella and Lucy are in a great deal of trouble now. I cannot imagine why they thought this was a sensible idea.'

Sophia held the Mars Bar out to Reverend Mother, who took it quickly and glided out of the room. Sophia thought she heard the sounds of coughing and chortling outside the door before all went quiet again.

Meanwhile in the dormitory upstairs in Slum Alley, nuns had magically drifted in from all directions to deal with the offenders and take them immediately to face Sister Francis in her office.

'Arabella!' Sister Francis said, 'you are head girl! Did we make a mistake? You have shown no responsibility whatsoever. And you, Lucy . . . as deputy head girl, it is your responsibility to help Arabella.'

'But Sister Francis,' Lucy began, 'I was helping her.'

'You know exactly what I am talking about,' Sister Francis said, glaring angrily at the two girls and reminding them why she was known as Sister Frowncis amongst the pupils.

'Why, at any point one of you could have fallen from the window on to the drive below and that really doesn't bear thinking about, does it? I mean, what would I have said to your parents?'

'Sorry,' Arabella mumbled, looking at the bare floorboards beneath her feet.

'Sorry, Sister Francis,' Lucy echoed.

'We won't do it again,' Arabella added.

'You are dismissed,' Sister Francis said, 'while I think of a suitable punishment, though what the best punishment is for dangling confectionery out of a third floor window and enticing an invalid to lean out of the infirmary is, I have no idea because this sort of thing has simply never happened before at Shaston.'

'I bet it has,' Arabella said cheerfully to Lucy as they both hared along the corridors, eager to tell their friends what had happened.

'At least we haven't been expelled,' Lucy said. 'My sister was expelled and my parents were pretty cheesed off about that.'

The legend of the Mars Bar became wildly popular among the girls and helped to lift their spirits at the beginning of a rather dull January.

* * *

Rosie and David avoided each other as much as they could, only communicating when they absolutely had to in choir rehearsals or greeting each other with a curt 'Good morning' when passing in the corridor.

'Crumbs, Rosie,' Grace said one morning at break, 'what's up with you and David? You seem to have fallen out big time and it's only the second week of term. What's wrong?'

'Thought you'd be pleased,' Rosie answered. 'You did warn me off David at the end of last term, when he said he'd give me a ticket for his recital.'

'I didn't mean you should cut him dead whenever you met!' Grace exclaimed. 'He's a great bloke, we've been friends for years, but I didn't think he was right for you, well, for anyone if I'm honest, not knowing what I do. Some people are better off staying single and he's one of them.'

'I thought you might be interested in him,' Rosie said, 'for yourself. I saw you both in Shaston the day after the end of term. I was in a coffee shop and you were both chatting outside, though if I'm honest you looked as if you were giving him a piece of your mind.

'And there's the graffiti I found, on the wall in the undercroft. It says Donna loves David and that you do as well.'

Grace let out a guffaw of laughter which had several heads swivelling in their direction in the staff room.

'As if I would be interested in David Hart,' she said, when she had finally stopped cackling. 'Hey, you're serious, aren't you? And you're upset. Tell you what, this isn't the best place to chat about personal stuff. Why don't you come over to mine for supper one evening?

'I'll tell you exactly what I was saying to David when I bumped into him in Shaston and a lot more besides.

'By the way,' she added, 'I've some romantic news of my own that I've been keeping under wraps. His name's Roberto and he's gorgeous.'

'I'd love to come to supper and I can't wait to hear about your mystery man. Why didn't you mention him before?'

'I thought I did,' Grace said. 'Remember when I told you about making a stocking for someone I was fond of, the Christmas before last? That was for Roberto.'

'Ah,' Rosie said, comprehension dawning. 'I thought you meant David.'

'We need to get down to some serious gossip. Is tomorrow too soon?'

'Perfect. And if you don't mind, I'll tell you all about what happened in the holidays, at David's recital. I might burst if I don't tell someone about it soon.'

'Can't wait,' Grace said, 'and obviously anything you tell me will go no further.'

'Likewise. Now, duty calls — I'm off to teach Clementine.'

Sitting at the piano in one of the music rooms, Rosie's fingers picked out a jaunty tune as she waited for her pupil.

'Ah, there you are, Clementine! I thought you'd forgotten your lesson.'

Rosie smiled as Clementine rushed into the room, bright red in the face with her hair escaping from her plait.

'Is everything all right?'

Clementine nodded uncertainly.

'Sure? OK then, come and sit down. I'm so proud of you. You've done really well in your Grade One. I have the mark sheet here. Shall we read it through together and see what we can learn from it?'

Rosie closed the lid of the piano and spread the mark sheet out in front of the two of them. Clementine blinked furiously in a vain attempt to read the comments.

'They are rather hard to read, aren't they?' Rosie said sympathetically. 'I can hardly make out the writing myself.'

Gracious, she thought. I know doctors have poor handwriting, but this music examiner's script reminds me of a crazed spider that has fallen into a bottle of ink and run all over the page.

Once she had finally deciphered the words and read them out to Clementine, they set to learning a new piece, then sight-read a duet with a jazzy feel.

As they came to the triumphant ending, the door opened and David stood there smiling at Clementine.

'Well done to you, Clemmie,' he said. 'I've just heard how well you did in Grade One. Your mum and dad are going to be so pleased. And that duet sounded fabulous. Well done to you too, Miss Peach.'

Rosie nodded.

'It was all down to Clementine's hard work. She's so easy to teach.'

'Uncle David helped me, too,' Clementine piped up. 'He always wants to hear me play when I see him at the weekends and he's always asking about you, Miss Peach. Lots and lots of questions.'

It was David's turn to look embarrassed then and he said his goodbyes and made off hastily.

'What does Mr Hart ask about me?' Rosie said to Clementine once the door was firmly shut.

'What happens in the lessons, what you say, if you look happy, everything really.'

'I see,' Rosie said. She wondered why David was so interested in her when he had turned away from her in such an offhand way after his recital in December.

I must have done something to provoke the situation, Rosie thought, but I have no idea what it was. We had been getting on together so well before that it seemed particularly unkind of him and yet now he has popped into Clementine's lesson as if nothing was wrong.

'Sometimes Uncle David is sad,' Clementine offered. 'Mummy and Daddy say so but they don't know what to do about it. Shall we play the duet again?'

'Good idea,' Rosie said, grateful to move away from an awkward topic.

'Will you count us in this time?'

Clementine giggled as she and Rosie romped through the lively piece.

'I don't want to go back to class now,' Clementine said.

'Oh, but you must,' Rosie said. 'Your teacher, Miss Browning, is going to explain to your class how to use commas correctly. I know that because she was talking about it in the staff room at break.'

'I like punctuation,' Clementine said, 'but I don't want to walk back to class on my own. Will you walk with me?'

'Of course I will.' Rosie smiled at Clementine.

She's so good at the piano and so bright, thought Rosie, that sometimes I forget she's only six.

But Rosie had a sneaking suspicion something was worrying Clemmie today. She'd never been late for a lesson before and she was usually more than happy to make her own way back to her classroom. She would mention it to one of the nuns.

* * *

Grace went round to Rosie's lodgings to collect her in her car the next evening.

'It'll be so much easier for you,' Grace had explained earlier. 'You don't want to be cycling over through the country lanes at night and it only takes a few minutes for me to pick you up. I'll drop you back home later. No, honestly, it's fine. I insist.'

'Hello,' Rosie said as she greeted Grace on the doorstep of the Fields' house. 'I'm running a bit behind. Would you like to pop up and see my room while I get myself together?'

'Definitely,' Grace said. 'I'm always interested in seeing where other people live; naturally nosy, that's me!'

Grace followed Rosie up the three staircases of the large house, with friendly greetings from various members of the Field family they encountered on the way up.

'Bit of a rabbit warren, isn't it?'

Grace whispered. 'How many children do the Fields have? Oh, your room is lovely. Great view from up here and you've made everything look so pretty.'

'I enjoy living here, although it can get a bit lonely. This is where I cook my meals,' Rosie said, pointing to a Baby Belling cooker in the corner, next to a tiny sink. 'I use the family bathroom downstairs. It's a bit of a trek and there's a queue in the morning but we have a timetable and I've got used to being very quick.'

'I started off in a bedsit a bit like this,' Grace said. 'I'm lucky now to have my own cottage. Mum and Dad helped me out a lot and of course it gives them somewhere to stay when they come over to England, which is useful.'

Clarifications – and a Warning

'Wow, this is fabulous!' Rosie said when Grace proudly showed her the tiny terraced cottage she lived in. 'It's a real home. Love the cushions — and the kitchen! Maybe once I've been teaching a few more years, I could think about getting a place of my own.'

'Come and sit down,' Grace said. 'I've got a few snacks and what about a drink?'

'Lovely,' Rosie answered. 'Something smells awfully good in your kitchen.'

'Chilli con carne,' Grace said, 'the only meal I know how to cook! Now, tell me about this recital you went to, David's recital, at Christmas.'

Rosie took a big breath and told Grace everything, beginning with how she had arrived at St Stephen's in the morning and heard David practising, right up to the moment when David had cruelly turned away from her after the concert.

'So you see, after that, Tristan gave me a lift home and I still don't understand what David was so mad about,' Rosie said.

'Tell me more about Tristan.'

'He was in my year at college. He's a friend although he tries it on a bit sometimes which can be annoying,' Rosie explained, 'but that evening when he dropped me at my parents' house, he didn't make any of his usual comments or pester me at all.

'He actually looked quite upset and kept saying he was sorry. Once he had seen me to the door, he gave me a pat on the shoulder, then left.'

'Do you think . . . ' Grace began. 'No, forget it — that would be ridiculous.'

'What?' Rosie asked.

'I just thought, what if David had seen you leaving with Tristan? Would he have been jealous?'

'But he made it perfectly clear he didn't want me hanging around. He said he'd see me next term.'

'But you said he had previously asked you to see him after the recital,' Grace reminded Rosie.

'He obviously changed his mind,' Rosie said. 'He can be very changeable — have you noticed? Anyway, he wouldn't have seen me leaving with Tristan because it was snowing and Tristan drove after me.

'I presume David was inside the church with all his admirers. Mind you, I have to say he played absolutely brilliantly. It was the best organ recital I've ever been to.'

'David can be jealous,' Grace said, 'at least that's what Donna used to say.'

'What were you talking to David about in Shaston when I saw you?' Rosie asked.

'I was telling him not to string you along,' Grace said. 'I had a few hours before I had to leave for the airport so I popped into town. Dad always has a list of things he wants me to take over — Marmite, teabags, his favourites you can't get over there, and who should I bump into but David?

'I had been thinking about him inviting you to the recital and how I had warned you he wasn't quite what he seemed and so when I saw him I couldn't help myself. I told him to leave you alone unless he was sure it would be different from how it was with Donna.'

'And I thought you were trying to stop him seeing me because you wanted him for yourself,' Rosie said. 'What a tangled web it all is! You haven't explained the graffiti in the undercroft though.'

Grace roared with laughter.

'I can't believe you managed to find that and then, what's more, took a few scratchings on the wall seriously! When I wrote that I was about fourteen years old and had a crush on David, as we all did. It meant nothing then and it still means nothing.'

'What about Roberto?' Rosie asked. 'You did say you'd tell me about Roberto.'

'I can do better than that,' Grace said. 'Here he is in this photo. Isn't he divine?'

Rosie admired the photograph of Grace's family and friends standing in a semi-circle at Christmas in Rome. One of the tall dark young men had his arm draped across Grace's shoulder and was gazing at her adoringly.

'Roberto is the man of my dreams. I think about him all the time,' Grace said. 'I've waited so long for this to work out. Now, are you ready for pudding?

'I thought being in love was supposed to make you lose your appetite but I'm ravenous. I cheated and bought some cream cakes from the bakery in Shaston.'

'I love that shop,' Rosie said. 'It's one of my favourite haunts, that and Hine and Parson's.'

'I love Hine and Parson's, too,' Grace said. 'I've bought so much wool there over the years. I only have to go into the shop and see their displays to get inspired to knit.'

Rosie and Grace were the best of friends by the end of the evening and when Rosie went to sleep that night she thought that although nothing had changed between her and David, at least she had a good friend to confide in.

Now she had to try to accept what Grace had told her — namely, that she was better off without David.

But my heart aches for him, Rosie thought. It's going to be difficult, impossible even, to forget him.

* * *

Sister Anthony soon sold out of Mars Bars in the tuck shop she ran on Sunday afternoons and girls kept the empty wrappers to present to Arabella and Lucy as tokens of respect. They amassed quite a collection, which helped to make up for the many and various punishments Sister Francis had devised for them.

'I can't believe we have to help with the washing up again,' Arabella moaned one evening after supper.

'We should only be doing this once a term, like the others,' Lucy grumbled, 'but this is the third time this week.'

The washing up machine at Shaston School was a sight to behold. The mighty contraption could have been designed by Heath Robinson himself, such was its size and complexity.

Arabella and Lucy donned cotton aprons and began loading dirty plates into racks which then travelled at speed on a sort of helter skelter towards an enormous aluminium shed resembling a car wash.

Once inside, the plates were subjected to vigorous and intensely noisy cleaning with scalding hot water and chemical-smelling soap suds before travelling off on the metal tracks towards the drying section.

It was a struggle to keep up with the appetite of the fearsome beast for dirty crockery and Arabella and Lucy felt quite worn out by the end of the session.

'I say, let's go to the sixth form common room for some toast,' Arabella suggested as the two girls made their way down the corridor. 'We deserve it after doing all that work.'

'But we've been banned from the common room,' Lucy said nervously.

'We've been banned from almost everything,' Arabella said in disgust. 'Weekend television, tuck shop, using the phone, exeats . . . not sure we're even allowed to breathe, are we?'

'I'm sorry for what we did,' Lucy said. 'Really sorry, although I think we cheered Sophia up no end.'

'I'm sorry, too,' Arabella said.

'In that case,' Sister Francis said as she stepped out of the shadows with a beatific smile on her face, 'I suggest you both go and enjoy some tea and toast in the common room with your friends. You have been punished enough. That is my final word on the subject.'

'Yippee,' Arabella screamed as she shot upstairs to the sixth form common room and pulled a couple of slices of what the girls referred to as 'Mother's Shame' out of a plastic packet and stuck them in the toaster.

'I'll make the tea,' Lucy said as she rammed the plug into the electric kettle, hastily disconnecting the appliance again to fill it with water when a strange parched hissing noise occurred.

'Nutella or jam?' Arabella asked, holding up two different jars of spread and shaking them like maracas.

'Both,' Lucy replied.

* * *

'David? Hi. It's Isobel here.'

'Hello, Isobel,' David said. 'Sorry, it took me ages to get to the phone. I was playing the piano and didn't hear the ringing at first.'

'Good job your nearest neighbours are only the cows in the fields outside your cottage,' Isobel said. 'I know how loudly you can play when you're in one of your moods! And that's why I've rung you, in a roundabout sort of way.'

'Because I have moods?' David asked. 'Fine sister you are!'

'I know you're teasing, so you can stop straight away.' Isobel cleared her throat. 'The thing is, David, Rod and I, well and Mum too, we're all worried about you.'

'No need.'

'I think there is. You're upset about something — you have been ever since your recital back in December. What is it? You know you can talk to me about any topic under the sun, don't you?'

'Post-Christmas slump, that's all,' David mumbled. 'Happens to a lot of musicians. We're frantically busy then there's nothing except grey skies and drizzle.'

'The weather's been quite good,

actually,' Isobel persisted. 'Spring flowers beginning to push through at last, lighter evenings . . . Oh, why don't you come round to lunch this weekend and maybe we'll go for a nice long walk and have a chat? Please?'

'I'd love to,' David said. 'You are very kind. But I'm not promising to bare my soul or tell you all my secrets.'

I can't share my secrets with anyone, David thought as he put the phone down. He made himself a coffee, then sat looking at old photos in his album, photos of him and Donna getting engaged, wedding photos, holidays, photos of the two of them in the cottage.

We had such a short time together, he thought. Everyone thinks I'm crazy with grief, but it's much more complicated than that. Of course I'm sorry she died, but it released me, released me from a terrible situation.

David slammed the book shut. I'll talk to Isobel, he thought as he went back to his piano and played a mournful melody, his fingers caressing the keys.

Love and Loss

Sophia eased her shoes off her feet and tried to listen to what Miss Browning was saying about one of their set works for English A level.

'I particularly love this Tennyson quotation,' Miss Browning was saying, 'about love and loss. ' 'Tis better to have loved and lost than never to have loved at all.' '

There was a general sigh from the class at this point. Almost any discussion of love would have the girls' imaginations running riot, but when it was connected with loss as well, it was totally overwhelming.

'How tragic,' Arabella said.

'Devastating,' Lucy murmured.

'My toes itch so much,' Sophia said.

'What did you say, Sophia?' Miss Browning asked in a concerned voice. 'Are you quite well? I know you have been out of circulation for a while with your illness.'

'Please don't talk about circulation. I've got chilblains,' Sophia moaned. 'It was so cold in the infirmary. They're really itchy so I've taken my shoes off.'

Arabella held her nose.

'You needn't think you're the only one who's been freezing to death,' she said. 'The nuns seem to have turned the heating off everywhere. They think it's spring already.'

'Used to be much worse, though,' Lucy chipped in. 'Remember two years ago, when we had the three-day week? No heating, no power, in the depths of winter. I had chilblains then. They wouldn't heal and I had to go around the school wearing my slippers for weeks.'

'I thought it was romantic, doing our homework by candlelight.' Arabella flopped back in her chair and ran her fingers through her thick dark curls, adopting a dramatic pose.

'The school was like an ice box,'

Sophia said. 'If the radiators ever came on, we used to fight to sit on them, that is, until Sister Anthony told us we'd get piles.' She grinned.

'I asked her what piles were and she wouldn't tell me,' Arabella said, giggling hysterically now.

'Maybe we could imagine what day-to-day life was like in Victorian times for Tennyson and Keats, without the benefit of central heating or electric lighting?' Miss Browning suggested in a desperate attempt to get the discussion back to the Romantic Poets they were meant to be studying.

'Honestly, Rosie,' Grace said at lunch later, 'those girls take any opportunity to try to divert the lesson. Pass me the mashed potato, would you? I'm . . . '

'I know, you're starving.' Rosie said. 'You always are!'

'I eat as much as I can at school lunch,' Grace confided, 'then I don't have to cook in the evening. Bit of cheese on toast, something like that is fine for supper.'

'I'd love to have the chance to do more cooking,' Rosie said. 'The options are limited on my Baby Belling, although I've managed to make lasagne. Took ages though and I did wonder if it was really worth it for one person.'

'That reminds me. I've been thinking . . . ' Grace said. 'How would you like to move in with me and be my lodger? I've got the spare room lying empty and we could have a lot of fun. You could teach me how to cook. It's time I learned how to make something other than chilli con carne.'

'Wow!' Rosie said. 'I'd love to. I'd pay you the usual rent, of course. I enjoy living with the Fields and they were so kind to offer me a home when I first moved to Dorset, but maybe it's time to move on. I could speak to them tonight and ask if they want much notice.'

'Great idea. Should suit us both!'

'You'll do,' David said as he carefully picked a snowdrop. He was trying to pick the flowers that were growing in out of the way places in his garden so there would still be plenty left there on view, bobbing their heads and dancing in the fresh breeze.

There! A decent bunch for Isobel and I'd better pick a few more to make a posy for Clemmie, too, David thought, waving at an inquisitive cow who was staring at him from the next door field.

'Climb every mountain . . . ' David sang. It was a family tradition started by his mother Valerie to sing this song from 'The Sound of Music' when you were in a situation that required a boost of self-confidence.

'Search high and low,' David continued. He was dreading talking to his sister but also couldn't wait to unburden himself.

It's been too long, he thought. I've kept this secret too long.

* * *

'Uncle David! Uncle David!' Clementine danced round him in a circle as he came through the front door of Isobel and Rod's cottage.

'Careful,' Valerie said, 'you'll trip David up, dancing around like that.'

'Hello, Mum. I didn't know you were going to be here for lunch, too. What a lovely surprise. Hi, Rod, keeping well? And Clemmie, I've some snowdrops for you, from my garden.'

'Thank you,' Clementine said, still dancing around. 'I've learned another piece on the piano. With Miss Peach.'

'I look forward to hearing that,' David said, then wandered off to the kitchen to say hello to Isobel and put the flowers in water.

The unmistakeable smell of roast lamb and rosemary filled the kitchen.

'Can I do anything?' David asked. 'Lay the table or chop something?'

'All done,' Isobel said with a smile. 'What lovely flowers! And don't look at me like that. I'm not going to interrogate you in front of Mum.'

'Thank goodness for that,' David said. 'So, I'm off the hook?'

'Certainly not,' Isobel replied. 'You

and I are going for a long walk after lunch while Rod washes up, and Mum and Clemmie watch a film. It's all arranged.'

'I know when I'm beaten,' David said sorrowfully, wiping away mock tears.

'Idiot!' Isobel said affectionately before swatting him with the tea towel.

'That lamb was perfect,' David said at the end of the meal.

'And the apple pie was to die for,' Rod added. 'I'm so glad I married you, Isobel.'

'Mummy isn't only a cook,' Clementine said.

'They know that, darling Clemmie,' Isobel said. 'They're both teasing, that's all.'

'Teasing isn't nice.' Clementine scratched the tablecloth and started kicking her chair leg rhythmically. 'Arabella said so.'

'Who's Arabella?' Isobel asked. 'Is she in your class?'

'No, Arabella is a big girl,' Clementine said.

'Do you mean Arabella the head girl?' David pulled Clementine on to his knee. 'What is it, Clemmie? Has someone been teasing you?'

'Yes, they have. They've been calling me a nasty name for ages and ages and chasing me when I didn't want them to. I said, 'Stop it' lots of times but they wouldn't. They said not to tell but I told Arabella yesterday and she said it was horrid teasing and it wasn't very nice.'

A big fat tear rolled down Clementine's rosy cheek and she wriggled free from David and ran to her mother, hiding her face in her lap and crying as if her heart would break.

'What did they call you, sweetheart?' Isobel asked.

'Carrot head!' Clementine sobbed.

'I used to get called that at school,' Valerie said, patting her hair which was now completely grey. 'You should be proud of your red hair — it's beautiful.'

'Sometimes they pull my hair and

push me on the floor. They did it yesterday.'

'Who did?' Rod said sternly. 'This is very wrong.'

'No-one is allowed to treat you like that,' Isobel said. 'That's not teasing, it's bullying. You've done the right thing, telling us. What's the girl's name, the one that's been tormenting you?'

'Can't say,' Clementine whispered. 'She told me not to. She said she'd cut off my plait if I squealed on her.'

'But you told Arabella?'

'Not the name, only what they did, all the times they called me Carrot Head and chased me and pushed me. She said she would tell Sister Francis and all the nuns and then it would stop but that was at the end of school yesterday and nothing's happened. I don't want to go to school next week.'

'You come with me,' David said. 'Why don't we play the piano together for a while and Granny can be our audience? Maybe your mum and dad would like to have a chat with each other in the kitchen?'

The phone in the hall rang as he was speaking and Isobel ran to answer it.

'Hello? Reverend Mother? No, not at all, in fact I was rather hoping to talk to you. Clementine has only this minute told us an alarming story about . . .

'Ah, yes, I'm so glad you know about that . . . of course I do understand the girl concerned must be very unhappy to have behaved so badly and yet I . . . Yes, Arabella is a very responsible girl to have passed on the information to you . . . I see . . . '

David closed the door to the hall gently and sat down at the piano.

'What about making up a piece, Clemmie? You're so good at that.'

Within a few minutes Clementine was improvising a simple piece at the top of the piano, with David vamping a bass part to fit.

'Encore,' Valerie said. 'You're a real little musician, Clemmie.'

'Cup of coffee, anyone?' Rod said, coming through from the kitchen with a large tray. 'There's some milk for you, Clemmie. Maybe you'd like to pass round those yummy chocolates Granny brought for us all.'

'Chocolate!' Clementine screamed. 'Sorry for shouting, Daddy,' she added quickly.

'You can do what you want today,' Rod said. 'Come here for a hug.'

Isobel came back into the sitting-room, wreathed in smiles, but with her mascara running a little under her eyes.

'Reverend Mother is a very wonderful woman,' she said. 'It's all sorted and you won't be getting any more trouble, Clemmie.

'Reverend Mother says she is so sorry this has happened to you but she doesn't want you to worry any more. It's over. The certain young lady who was unkind to you is on her way home to her parents right now.

'Apparently she has been terrorising lots of the little ones, took pleasure in it, in fact.'

'I didn't tell you her name,' Clementine said in bewilderment.

'You didn't need to — she has admitted what she did to you when Reverend Mother was tackling her about something else,' Isobel said.

'What a nasty bully!' Valerie said. 'Good riddance to her, that's what I say.'

'Arabella had the sense to pass on what Clemmie told her to Reverend Mother and it all fitted as part of a much bigger picture, with information from other girls and from staff.

'The girl concerned had been warned before about her behaviour and this was the last straw,' Isobel said. 'She's been expelled. We probably don't need to say any more about it for now.'

'Quite,' Valerie said. 'Little pitchers and all that.'

'Would you like to watch a film with me, Clemmie?' Valerie asked. 'On the sofa? I think Daddy's going to wash up and Uncle David's going for a walk with your Mummy.'

'Look what's on! 'The Sound of Music'!' Clementine's eyes lit up.

'My favourite,' Valerie said. 'Perfect timing. Now, pass the chocolates round, there's a dear.'

* * *

Isobel and David walked in silence down the country lanes then across a field and up to one of their favourite walks, high up on the hill. Each of them was reluctant to start the conversation they knew they must have, namely, the conversation about Donna.

'I know Donna was a close friend of yours, Isobel . . . ' David began at last.

'I can see it's like Clemmie being bullied, in a way . . . ' Isobel said at the same time, then brother and sister laughed.

'You first,' David said.

'OK,' Isobel said. 'Here goes. Promise not to be offended by anything I say?'

'Promise,' David replied. 'Likewise?'

'Pact,' Isobel and David said at the same time as they linked their little fingers together in a ritual they had been doing since early childhood.

'Donna was a lovely friend to us all at school,' Isobel began.

'I know, I know,' David interrupted impatiently. 'You don't need to tell me what a great person she was — you and Donna were practically inseparable for years.'

'David, you need to listen to me,' Isobel said. 'Don't speak until I've finished. OK?'

David nodded his assent as his sister continued.

'You remember that summer she asked me down to stay at her parents' house in Totnes? Well, I saw a different side of her then. I don't know what was wrong, but she seemed in a strange mood the whole time I was there.

'I wanted to come home after a few days, even rang Mum and Dad, begging them to collect me, but they wouldn't hear of it. They thought I was being a spoilt brat, I suppose.

'The strange thing was, I couldn't bring myself to tell them why I wanted to come home.' She hesitated for a moment. 'I felt a loyalty to Donna so I said I felt homesick, which was true, but not the whole truth. Mum and Dad didn't think that was a good enough reason to let me return, after all I was fifteen — too old to be homesick.

'They didn't want to be impolite to Donna's parents, either, so I stayed for the full week. I've never been as glad as I was when I got home at the end of it.'

'I have a vague recollection of Mum saying you had missed home more than she thought you would,' David said. 'She used to say afterwards she was glad she hadn't let you become a boarder because she didn't think you were suited to it. So what went wrong that week? How did Donna behave?'

'For starters, she read my diary,' Isobel said. 'I stayed in the spare room in her parents' house and kept my diary by the bed. It was one of those leather bound five-year diaries, like a miniature old-fashioned volume from an ancient library, with a gold-coloured padlock.'

'The one Mum and Dad gave you at Christmas? You loved that diary. Did you forget to lock it?'

'No, I didn't and even if I had, it was totally wrong of her to read it. You don't do that sort of thing. Donna picked the lock of my diary. She broke in and read my most private thoughts then locked it again.'

'Did she mention what she had read?' David asked.

'No, not once,' Isobel said.

'Are you absolutely sure she picked the lock and read it?' David asked.

'Absolutely,' Isobel said grimly, 'because she wrote nasty comments on the pages. She read my private secrets and scrawled unpleasant remarks in her writing all over my precious diary.

'I knew she was able to pick a lock because the previous term at school she had spent ages teaching herself how to. She wanted to get into Sister Anthony's tuck shop cash box to take some of the money.

'She said Sister Anthony had given her the wrong change one day. Sister Anthony said she was mistaken, then Donna became obsessed with getting into the cash box and retrieving the money she said she was owed. We all thought it was hilarious and totally believed her.'

'Did she manage to pick the lock of the cash box?' David asked.

'Yes, but of course Sister Anthony knew what was going on. They always seemed to know everything that was going on.'

'They haven't changed,' David said. 'They would give the secret service a run for their money.'

'I can believe that,' Isobel replied with a smile. 'Anyway, Sister Anthony sent for Donna and 'had a word' when she discovered the tuck box had money missing. Donna came back white in the face after that and refused to talk about it.'

'Did you tackle Donna about reading your diary when you stayed with her?' David asked.

'No. I was so shocked and hurt. It sounds weird, I know, but I couldn't talk to her about it.'

'It doesn't sound weird to me,' David said. 'It sounds familiar. What else happened during the week in Devon?'

'Nothing much, on the surface, at least, but I didn't trust her after that. I noticed a couple of occasions when I heard her tell her mother a deliberate lie about where we had been during the day and the lies seemed pointless.

'For example, one day she told her mother we had been to a particular café on the beach to get ice-cream when in fact we'd gone into town and had ice-cream in a teashop. I didn't know why she had bothered to lie — her parents hadn't forbidden us to go into town or anything like that. She seemed to lie for the sheer fun of it.'

David's face darkened.

'You should have told Mum and

Dad,' he said. 'I hate to think of you being unhappy and bottling stuff up. You could have told me.'

'I don't know why I didn't,' Isobel said. 'I suppose I wanted things to go back to normal, after all she was my friend. Once term started again, Donna took me aside and said she was sorry about not being nice to me in the summer holidays.

'She told me she had been silly and thoughtless and begged me to forgive her. She asked if I had mentioned it to anyone in my family and was pleased when she found I hadn't.'

'You said it was like Clemmie being bullied,' David said. 'Do you mean Donna bullied you?'

'No, that's not it exactly. It's more that the situation with Clemmie this morning made me think about how I should have told Mum and Dad why I didn't want to stay in Totnes with Donna and her family all those years ago,' Isobel said. 'I'm proud of Clemmie for speaking out, even if it was

Arabella she told first.'

'But you remained friends with Donna,' David said. 'I remember coming home from music college at the end of the summer term and finding you, Donna and countless other sixth formers from Shaston sitting in the garden one glorious June evening. You had all just finished your A levels and were celebrating with a barbecue.'

'Yes, that was a great party,' Isobel said. 'But although Donna and I remained part of the same group of friends, it was never quite as it had been before. I didn't trust her in the same way. She'd hurt me too much.'

'That party, the barbecue,' David said, 'that was the evening I fell in love with Donna.'

Isobel sighed.

'I know Donna meant everything to you David and that's why I warned you at the beginning of our talk that you might be offended by what I had to say.'

David took quite a few long angry strides before he spoke.

'Nothing you could ever say would offend me. You think I was happy with Donna — everyone does, especially Mum. You think I won't let myself fall in love again because I miss her too much. None of it is true. Being married to Donna was, well, let's say it was difficult, almost impossible at times.'

'David!' Isobel exclaimed. 'Why didn't you say anything?'

'How could I? I felt so bewildered and confused. As soon as we were married, I began to see another side to Donna; I don't want to go into details, but I suspected she was deceiving me.'

'You mean . . . ?' Isobel said, aghast to suspect her sister-in-law of infidelity.

David hung his head.

'I confronted her but she laughed in my face and said she could see who she liked and that our marriage meant nothing to her. Later she calmed down and said was sorry, she had made up some stupid lies and that she loved me.

'She said she was trying to test my love, to see whether I cared if she was unfaithful and of course she would never betray me.

'I mentioned to Mum we'd argued and she said it always seems like the end of the world when a young couple have their first disagreement and I should forget it, that Donna was the perfect wife for me and I was lucky to have her.

'But afterwards I began to be stupidly jealous and checked up on her endlessly, asking why she was back from work late, where had she been, all that sort of thing and then . . . '

'Then the tragedy,' Isobel said. 'The car crash. Donna's death.'

'She was on her way home that evening after work. The roads were icy, with poor visibility. You know all this, Isobel. I don't need to tell you how she died.'

'Never mind,' Isobel said. 'Go on. Get it off your chest. Tell me the whole story as if I were a stranger.'

'Donna was driving along a tiny winding coastal road. There were some sort of road works on the main route and traffic was diverted, so it wasn't her usual route and she wouldn't have been used to the bends in the road in the dark, especially in poor driving conditions and the car went over . . . I can't bear to think of it.

'At least Donna was killed outright and didn't have to suffer, beyond a quick moment of terror. My darling beautiful Donna, dead. I still had feelings for her, despite our differences. For a long time she had meant the world to me.'

Isobel paused on the grassy track and held David in her arms.

'Maybe Donna wasn't concentrating,' David said, his voice muffled as he clung to his sister. 'Maybe she was distracted because of something I had said, my stupid jealousy. I'll never know the complete truth of what happened, how she spent her last few seconds. I blame myself. Who else is there to blame, with Donna gone?'

'You'll feel better for telling me all

this,' Isobel said. 'And you have to stop blaming yourself. It was a tragic accident.

'I can't let myself fall in love again,' David whispered, his shoulders heaving with the pent-up emotion of his long-buried secret. 'I was no good as a husband.'

'Time to walk back,' Isobel said softly. 'The others will be wondering where we've got to. You may think you messed up being a husband first time round, but make sure you have a think about what I told you about Donna. She wasn't Miss Perfect by any means — no-one ever is.

'You deserve to find happiness with someone else. Besides, I'd like some nieces and nephews, so you'd better get a move on!'

David attempted a wan smile and began singing in a croaky voice:

'Climb every mountain, Search high and low . . . '

He felt a great weight lifting from his mind and his heart began to thaw.

Isobel finished off the chorus for him in her clear soprano voice:

'Follow every rainbow, Till you find your dream.'

Easter Holidays

'Look, Rosie,' Grace squealed as the plane circled to land at Fiumicino Airport, outside Rome. 'You can see the hills. The city's over there, in that direction.'

Grace pressed herself against her seat so that Rosie could have a clearer view out of the aeroplane window.

'I can't believe we're here,' Rosie said happily. 'You're so kind, asking me to join you and your family for Easter. What an adventure!'

'And to think,' Grace murmured, 'Roberto is down there somewhere, waiting to whisk us into Rome in his car.'

'You've got him well trained already,' Rosie said.

'He offered to collect us.' Grace flung herself forward to look out of the window again. 'I can't wait to see him.'

'I'll be wearing a green hairy suit most of the holiday, I think,' Rosie said.

'You what?' Grace looked puzzled, then suddenly burst out laughing. 'Oh, I see — you mean you'll be a gooseberry. I promise you it won't be like that.'

When Rosie and Grace finally strode out into the arrival hall, a tall good-looking young man started waving frantically.

'There he is! There's my Roberto,' Grace said as she abandoned her case on the floor and ran into his arms for a warm embrace.

Rosie felt a tiny pang then. If only, she thought, if only David was here to greet me like that. She pulled herself together quickly, telling herself not to spoil the moment but to make the best of her unexpected holiday.

Rosie had moved into Grace's cottage towards the end of the Easter term and the two of them had got on so well that an invitation to spend Easter in Rome had soon followed.

And here I am, Rosie thought in

amazement, in Italy for the first time, about to spend a lovely week with Grace and her family. I simply refuse to spoil it by thinking about David.

* * *

Meanwhile in Bath, Rosie's mother Sheila picked up the telephone.

'Rosie? Tristan here.'

'Hello? This is Sheila, Rosie's mother.'

'Oh, hello, Mrs Peach. This is Tristan. I was at college with Rosie.'

'Yes, Rosie has spoken of you,' Sheila said.

There was a slightly uncomfortable silence.

'Is Rosie there?' Tristan asked. 'May I speak to her?'

'I'm sorry to say you've missed her,' Sheila replied. 'She left this morning for a holiday in Rome with a good friend of hers. May I pass on a message?'

'Perhaps you wouldn't mind telling her I called to say I was sorry about, er, about, well, it doesn't matter now; it seems as if everything has worked out for her, so please don't bother to say anything about my call, unless of course you want to.'

When Sheila put the phone down, she felt a bit confused as to what she was or wasn't meant to say to Rosie. She certainly remembered Tristan from Rosie's college days and hoped he wasn't trying to bother her again.

Tristan felt mightily relieved at the end of the call. His conscience had been troubling him for quite some time, ever since David's recital in Bath, in fact.

When he had dropped Rosie home in the snow when she was so upset after the recital, Tristan realised he had overstepped the mark.

I really shouldn't have told David that Rosie and I had been an item at college, he thought to himself. It wasn't true, merely wishful thinking on my part, but also because it made David pretty mad, especially when I added the bit about how we were keen to rekindle our so-called relationship.

Tristan sat down and strummed a few chords on his piano.

I think I can recognise true love when I see it, he told himself, and I reckon David and Rosie love each other. They've obviously sorted everything out and gone for a romantic holiday in Rome. Good luck to them.

Tristan felt a sense of relief that his conscience was finally clear. He had interfered when he shouldn't have, but it was of no consequence now and all seemed to have worked out for the best.

He felt a little regretful when he realised Rosie was out of his reach now, but soon cheered up when he remembered he was taking a choir rehearsal that evening.

He thought he might ask one of the new altos to go for a drink with him in the pub afterwards. Who knew what that might lead to?

* * *

'This is where my parents first met,' Grace explained as she showed Rosie the beautiful writers' museum at the bottom of the Spanish Steps in Rome. Grace had been showing Rosie round the city for a few days now. She was proud of her home city and wanted to show Rosie her favourite places.

'Dad came over here as a young man,' Grace explained. 'He's always been fond of literature. I suppose that's where my love of English comes from. Anyway, he came to visit this museum when he was touring Europe with his friends. My mother was inside looking at various manuscripts.'

'Don't tell me,' Rosie said. 'Their eyes met across a crowded room and that was it: love at first sight.'

'That's pretty much it,' Grace said, 'at least that's what my dad says. He proposed within a few days but it took my mother a little longer to think he was the perfect match for her. She always thought she would marry an Italian, not an Englishman, but Dad persuaded her in the end.'

'Ah, how romantic,' Rosie said. 'My parents met when they both joined a choir. They still sing in the same choir, even now.'

'Let's hope we're both lucky enough to find lasting love,' Grace said, a special smile hovering around her lips. 'Now, shall we have a look upstairs? Keats actually lived here in the villa, in an apartment, until he died.'

'Aged twenty-five,' Rosie said with a shocked voice as she read her guide-book.

'All that talent lost,' Grace murmured. 'His life cut short by illness.'

Later that same afternoon, at home in her parents' apartment, Grace thought she would try to talk to Rosie about David again. She had something she wanted to show Rosie which might help her.

'Rosie, would you mind if we discussed David and his marriage again?' Grace asked. 'I don't want to upset you, so please say if you'd rather not.'

'All right,' Rosie said hesitantly. 'Do you know, I've been thinking about him, about David, today,' she admitted. 'Maybe it was reading about Keats dying so young, but the notion came to me that you've got to get on with life, not mope about. I need to resolve what I think about David and move on.'

'My thoughts exactly. You know I told you Donna had written to me when she was first married and told me she felt unhappy with David being jealous and so on? Well, I still have those letters here, in the flat.'

'Ah.'

'I'd like you to read one of them,' Grace said, 'that is, if you want to.'

'OK,' Rosie said, 'I think.'

'Have a look at this.' Grace took a letter out of an envelope and handed it to Rosie. 'Sit here on the balcony and read it while I put the kettle on for tea. Let me know what you make of it.'

A lot of the letter was about people and places Rosie didn't know, but one section in particular caught her attention.

'I feel so mixed up,' Rosie read. 'It's as if I was a girl again, when Isobel, David's sister, came to stay one summer. She seemed to turn against me. She never said anything but I felt she didn't like me any more, just because I played a few tricks. I said I was sorry when we got back to school, but I never felt she really trusted me after that. She has a very unforgiving nature.

'It's the same with David now. I said some silly things I regretted, nothing of any consequence, but he wasn't the same after that. He's so jealous and suspicious. I think he listens at the door when I'm on the phone and he's always asking me what time I'll be home, until I feel I have no freedom left . . . '

'Do you see what I mean?' Grace asked as she pattered on to the balcony with a welcome tray of tea. 'Here, have a mug.'

'Earl Grey,' Rosie said. 'I didn't

expect this in Rome.'

'My dad can't live without his Earl Grey. My mum still only drinks coffee though. I think the only thing she doesn't like about my dad is his tea habit.'

Rosie took a sip of the fragrant liquid.

'I thought the letter was interesting. She seems to think both David and Isobel turned against her at different times.'

'You're not saying she made it up?' Grace asked.

'No, of course not. It seems strange though, her thinking they both turned against her. Did Isobel ever mention going to stay with Donna in the holidays when you were all at school together?'

'Not in any derogatory way,' Grace said. 'Most of us in our friendship group stayed with each other at some time during our school years, although funnily enough I never stayed with Donna. She stayed here, though, one

Easter holiday. We had a great time.'

'Thanks for letting me see the letter. I'm not sure what I think at the moment. It's all a bit mystifying.'

Rosie hid her face with her mug as the memory of David kissing her passionately under the mistletoe at Shaston leaped into her mind unbidden.

Grace went over to hug Rosie.

'I know it's hard,' she whispered, 'but I don't think he's what you need.'

As Grace sat down again, she picked up the letter and read it. For the first time a tiny doubt crept into her mind about the accuracy of Donna's version of events.

Grace thought she knew Isobel really well but she didn't entirely recognise her in the account Donna had given.

Her thoughts were interrupted by a ring at door.

'Heavens,' Grace squealed as she found Roberto waiting outside. 'I can't believe it's so late. Rosie and I have been chatting and lost track of time. I was going to change before we all went out.'

'No need, *bellissima*,' Roberto said gallantly. 'You always look beautiful to me.'

'You flatterer!' Grace said with a laugh. 'Come out on to the balcony and have some tea while Rosie and I get ready. Promise we won't be long.'

'I'll pass on the tea,' Roberto said with a small shudder. 'I can't get used to this drink you love so much. Ah, hello, Rosie. It's so delightful to see you again.'

'Hello,' Rosie said shyly to Roberto. She hadn't seen him since he had given her and Grace a lift from the airport.

'Come on, Rosie,' Grace said, 'let's go and choose something suitable to wear to go out for a pizza. If you change your mind, Roberto, there's plenty of tea in the pot!'

Grace and Rosie hurried away, leaving Roberto sitting at the table with Donna's letter open in front of him. A light breeze blew the last page on to the tiled floor of the balcony and he bent over to retrieve it, folding the letter up and tucking it under the teapot.

He would never read a letter addressed to someone else, but couldn't help noticing Donna's extravagant signature at the end of the page.

Mmm, Donna, he said to himself. I remember that girl. She was Grace's friend who stayed here one Easter many years ago. She was trouble that holiday. What a tragedy she died, though. Poor Donna. She was a disturbed kid.

* * *

The evening at the local pizzeria was a great success. Roberto and Grace were joined by many of their friends for an entertaining evening.

'Pizzas taste different here,' Rosie said.

'I should hope so,' Roberto said. 'In fact I dread to think what an English pizza would taste like . . . '

'Don't be rude about the English,' Grace said.

'I wouldn't dare.' Roberto pretended to cringe in fear then laughed uproariously.

They're so happy together, Rosie thought. I do hope it works out for them.

Roberto walked Grace and Rosie back to the Brownings' apartment and stood there a little awkwardly as Grace opened the main door with her key.

'Tell you what,' Rosie said, 'I'll pop straight upstairs so you two lovebirds can say goodnight. See you in a minute, Grace.'

Grace shot her a grateful look and Rosie made her way to the lift inside the apartment block, leaving Roberto and Grace on the pavement. No way am I going to play gooseberry, she thought with a giggle.

Later, Grace tapped on Rosie's bedroom door.

'Rosie? May I come in? Oh, I've got so much to tell you, well, two things to tell you. It's so exciting!'

'Of course you can come in. I'm writing my parents a postcard.'

'The Spanish Steps — lovely,' Grace said. 'By the way, I'm engaged!'

Rosie threw her arms round Grace's neck.

'Wonderful, wonderful news!' she exclaimed. 'I had hoped that was on the cards. When did he ask you?'

'He asked me at Christmas,' Grace said, 'and I don't know how I've been able to keep it to myself all this time, but this evening I said yes to his proposal. I'm so happy!'

'It's obviously a family tradition,' Rosie said. 'You told me your mum took a long time to decide too.'

'Mum and Dad!' Grace said. 'I must go and tell them. Hang on though, what am I thinking of? There's something else and it concerns you.'

Rosie hoped Grace wasn't going to tell her one of Roberto's friends had taken a shine to her. She didn't feel up to having a new admirer right now.

'It's to do with Donna,' Grace continued. 'Roberto told me that when Donna stayed here years ago on holiday, when we were all teenagers, she tried to spoil things between us.'

'What did she do?' Rosie asked.

'Roberto said Donna lied to him about where she and I had gone one day, to make him think I was interested in another boy. By the time he found out she'd lied, I'd gone back to England, to school. He's never told me this before, but seeing Donna's letter on the balcony this afternoon reminded him.'

'How strange,' Rosie said.

'But don't you see, Rosie,' Grace burst out, 'it means you can't believe the letter. The more I think about it, the more contradictory it appears. I think I have to face it. Donna has misrepresented Isobel and David in that letter.'

'You mean . . . '

'Yes! David isn't the villain I thought he was. I'm so sorry, Rosie, I should never have tried to interfere between you.'

'Go and see your parents,' Rosie said, a smile lighting up her face. 'I have some serious thinking to do.'

By the morning, Rosie felt intense happiness for her friend Grace but also a glimmer of hope for herself. Maybe, she thought, her love story would have a happy ending, like Grace and Roberto's.

* * *

'I've got twenty-two,' Clementine said proudly.

'Twenty-two what?' David asked.

'Twenty-two Easter eggs.'

'You won't be needed this one then,' David said, bringing a massive egg decorated with a red bow from behind his back.

'Please!' Clementine shouted, making a lunge for the present. 'Some of my eggs are mini eggs so if you only count the big eggs, I've got five.'

'Still sounds like an awful lot for someone so small.' David shook his head. 'I think I should keep this one.'

'Hand it over, David,' Isobel advised. 'She's not going to give up.'

'It's brave of you to have us all over for Easter lunch,' Rod said.

'Thought it was my turn,' David said with a grin. 'Better pop into the kitchen, the timer's going off. Excuse me, all.'

Isobel, Rod, Valerie and Clementine sat for ages in the sitting-room waiting for David to return.

'What's that funny smell?' Clementine asked.

'Charcoal?' Rod suggested.

'I'll go and help,' Isobel said, nipping into the kitchen to see what could be salvaged.

'It's not too bad,' David said to her across a smoke-filled room. 'The water boiled dry in the vegetables, or possibly I forgot to put any water in the saucepan.'

'Where's the pan now?' Isobel asked.

'Honestly, David! You're so clever in some ways but in others, well, words fail me.'

Isobel filled the saucepan with water and put it outside the back door to be dealt with later.

'Have you had time to think about what we discussed?' Isobel asked as she dashed about the kitchen restoring order as best she could.

'What was that?' David asked.

'You know . . . Donna. Looking to the future.'

'Yes,' David said. 'Thank you. I feel a lot better about it. I'm beginning to realise it wasn't all my fault, the marriage failing.'

'She was a tricky person to be married to,' Isobel said firmly. 'Now, I'll pop some more veg on. Peas and carrots OK? Won't take long.'

'Mummy!' Clementine put her head round the kitchen door. 'It's getting late and it's past lunchtime. Granny said that. Just now.'

'Well, please thank Granny for her

comments,' Isobel said, 'and tell her it will be ten more minutes. And don't you dare start the eggs yet. They're for after lunch. Off you go now.'

'You mean she hasn't started her chocolate yet?' David asked. 'I know we used to start at breakfast.'

'I know she has but I have to pretend I don't know that. It's complicated being a parent,' Isobel explained.

'Sounds it,' David said. 'You know you said I should meet someone else?'

'Yes,' Isobel said, looking excited.

'I have met someone, at work. She's absolutely gorgeous but I've put her off with my stupid behaviour, blowing hot and cold, telling her I wasn't looking for anything serious.'

'Well, you need to get on with telling her how you really feel. What are you waiting for? If she's as gorgeous as you say, she won't be short of admirers.'

'It's too late.' David looked down at his feet. 'She's going out with someone else now, someone she used to go out with at college.

'That's why I was upset after the recital. I'd just found out from the man himself they were an item again. He said she was the love of his life.'

Isobel squeezed her brother's arm sympathetically.

'Oh, David, I'm so sorry. There'll be other chances. You wait and see.'

'I don't want other chances,' David said. 'I'm in love with Rosie.'

'Rosie?' Isobel said. 'Rosie Peach? Clemmie's piano teacher? She's adorable. You have so much in common with your music. In fact, I think Mum already has her earmarked for you.

'By the way, did you know Miss Peach told Reverend Mother ages ago that Clemmie seemed a little out of sorts in one of her piano lessons? That information was very useful when the horrible behaviour of that nasty bully was finally discovered. I wrote Miss Peach a note to thank her.'

'I didn't know that,' David replied, 'but it doesn't surprise me. Rosie is such a kind and thoughtful person.'

After a pause, he continued.

'But it doesn't change the fact that it's too late, for Rosie and me, I mean. She's going out with Tristan. I know she's gone abroad for Easter, not quite sure where. Maybe she's with Tristan right now.'

Isobel busied herself putting butter on the vegetables, her brain already darting this way and that to see how she could help her brother. At least she knew the name of David's beloved now.

When they had talked before, when she and David had gone for a long walk after their family roast lunch, she had suspected he was fond of someone but had decided against pushing him too hard for information.

I'll see what I can do about it next term, Isobel thought. David may be mistaken about this Tristan, whoever he is. There's always hope.

'Food's ready,' David called out as he plonked a casserole on to the table. 'Come and get it!'

'This is delicious, David,' Valerie said.

'Maybe a little more salt and perhaps you should have cut the meat smaller. The vegetables are lovely. Did you cook these, Isobel?'

'I like your cooking, Uncle David,' Clementine said, leaping to his defence. 'It's better than school dinners.'

'High praise indeed,' Rod said and everyone started to laugh.

'Happy Easter, everyone,' David said, raising his glass in a toast.

'Yes, happy Easter!'

'Happy Easter!'

And a happy Easter to you, my darling Rosie, wherever you are and whoever you're with, David thought.

The Temperature Rises

'Bother!' Lucy moaned as she threw a crumpled piece of blue linen on the floor. 'I can't get this seam to lie flat.'

'Let me see if I can help,' Arabella offered. 'I've nearly finished my dress — only the hem to go now.'

'I've cut the button holes too large in the bodice of my dress,' Sophia said unhappily. 'It's going to take ages to cobble this together with stitches and I'm running out of blue thread.'

'Here, have some of mine,' Arabella said. 'It doesn't quite match but it's good enough.'

The three sixth formers were frantically finishing off their uniform dresses on a Sunday afternoon at the beginning of the summer term.

It was school policy for the sixth formers to make their own uniform, consisting of an orangey brown tweed skirt for the winter and a pale blue linen dress for the summer.

The skirt and the dress could be of any design, but had to be made out of the regulation material supplied by the school. Reverend Mother had decreed that in view of the intensely hot weather, summer dresses could be worn from the beginning of the summer term instead of from half-term as usual and so the girls were keen to complete their sewing and put on cooler clothes.

'You girls should have finished these off last term,' Sister Anne said as she put her head round the needlework room door. 'How are you getting on?'

'I haven't quite finished because I was busy last term investigating the school bully,' Arabella reminded everyone.

'Yes, well done, Arabella,' Sister Anne remarked. 'You acted responsibly there. We knew then we had picked the right person to be head girl.'

'Sophia and I were helping Arabella,' Lucy said. 'We've been very busy. And

Sophia was ill last term, weren't you, Sophia?'

'I get the message,' Sister Anne said. 'You've all been busy. Now, Lucy, I think you are most in need of my help. Move over a bit at the sewing table, that's it. Give me your dress.'

With much tutting and a fair bit of chortling at Lucy's lack of skill as a seamstress, Sister Anne unpicked the faulty stitching, rethreaded the sewing machine properly and whizzed along the two edges of linen in record time, producing a highly professional-looking seam.

'Wow!' Lucy said in admiration. 'That is good.'

'I used to make clothes for my brothers and sisters in Ireland,' Sister Anne confided, 'when I was a young girl.'

'I've finished the hem!' Arabella shrieked. 'I can put my summer dress on at last and cool down!'

Arabella ran to the back of the sewing room where there was a tiny changing cubicle. She went in wearing an ill-fitting tweed skirt with baggy panels and emerged wearing a strangely misshapen blue linen dress with a wavy hemline.

'How do I look?' Arabella demanded.

'Ready for the summer,' Sophia said tactfully. 'Oh, Sister Anne, would you mind helping me with these wretched button holes?'

Within a couple of hours, all three girls had finished off their dresses and felt ready to resume their studies the next day feeling more comfortable in their lighter clothes.

'I say, aren't our A levels soon?' Arabella asked Sophia.

'Not sure,' Sophia replied. 'Miss Browning said something about an English exam this term, didn't she?'

'It will be fine,' Lucy said cheerfully. 'We've got ages and ages. The exams are weeks away. Why don't we walk down the drive in our new dresses?'

'Yeah!' Sophia jumped high into the air and one of the buttons flew off the bodice of her dress.

'I'll fix that for you later,' Sister Anne said as she scooped up the stray button. 'Be off with you now and have some fun.'

'We could nip into the tuck shop on the way,' Arabella suggested. 'Mars Bar, anyone?'

The three girls ran off giggling like mad, arms interlinked, while Sister Anne watched them proudly.

* * *

Tristan hummed to himself as he strode along the streets behind Selfridges in London, on his way to the Wigmore Hall. He was going to a lunchtime concert given by his former teacher, Fingerschmitt, and he was really looking forward to it.

Nearing the hall, he noticed a frail older lady struggling up the steps and offered her his arm.

'Please,' he said, 'allow me to help. Let me open the door for you.'

'Thank you, young man,' Miss Spiker said. 'I don't need to take your arm, but yes, if you'd care to hold the door open, I'd be grateful. I've had a long journey all the way from Dorset. I couldn't miss this recital. It's going to be such a treat.'

Tristan nipped up the steps and held the heavy glass door open for Miss Spiker with a flourish.

Inside, the atmosphere was electric, with seemingly half the pianists in England gathered to listen to the recital given by the famous maestro, Finger-schmitt.

You could hear a pin drop in the few seconds before the first piece started, such was the focus and anticipation of the audience.

Tristan gazed around at the pink marble and gold decorations of the concert hall. He always thought it felt quite decadent to be sitting in such a glorious room in the middle of the day and this made him enjoy the music even more.

In the interval, he chatted to hordes

of people he knew in the music world, circulating like a seasoned professional.

'Why, there you are again, young man,' a commanding voice at the height of his elbow rang out. Miss Spiker fixed him with a beady eye. 'What is your name?' she asked.

'Tristan Proudfoot, at your service.' Tristan gave Miss Spiker one of his most disarming smiles.

'Pleased to meet you, Tristan. I'm Dorcas, Dorcas Spiker. Thank you for helping me earlier. You know, I think I've heard your name before, it sounds familiar. Do you live in Dorset?'

'No, London,' Tristan replied. 'I'm a choral conductor.'

'Mmm,' Miss Spiker said. 'Adjudication?'

'Yes,' Tristan replied. 'I've done a few festivals. I was down in the West Country not so long ago, in fact.'

'That's it,' Miss Spiker said triumphantly. 'The music festival in Bath. Weren't you adjudicating? The school where I teach sent the school choir. I didn't go myself, but the girls and staff told me all about it. They were thrilled to be awarded second place and talked of nothing else for weeks.'

'Ah,' Tristan said, 'then I know which the school is — it's Shaston, in Dorset, isn't it? I happen to know Miss Peach. We were at college together.'

'A lovely young woman,' Miss Spiker said. 'She's taking on a lot more of my work now. I'm retiring soon, at the end of the term, in fact.'

'Really?' Tristan opened his eyes as wide as he could. 'You simply don't look old enough.'

Miss Spiker laughed uproariously and stood on tiptoes to dig Tristan in the ribs.

'I like you, Tristan. You're a hoot.'

Chatting away, the two musicians realised they had many acquaintances in common and an unlikely friendship was struck up between the pair of them, culminating in Miss Spiker asking Tristan to come to her retirement party in June.

'There'll be lots of musicians there,' she said. 'I'm allowed to ask a number of guests myself and of course most of the school will attend.'

'Sounds stupendous,' Tristan said. 'I'll put it in my diary. Thank you.'

'There is one thing, though,' Miss Spiker warned. 'All the musicians attending are required to play a party piece.'

'Well, it is a party,' Tristan quipped, 'so that makes sense.'

'Indeed,' Miss Spiker replied. 'You can sing, play the piano, or even do a comic turn, whatever you like.'

'What are you offering?' Tristan asked. 'Or are you let off because it's your party?'

'I'm playing my favourite piano piece in the world, the opening of the 'Moonlight Sonata',' Miss Spiker said. 'That's one of the reasons I was so keen to come to the concert today. Maestro Fingerschmitt's next piece in the recital is . . . '

' . . . the 'Moonlight Sonata'.' Tristan

smiled. 'I'm with you on that choice. However often you hear it, it still sounds fresh and new.'

'Time to go back for the second half,' Miss Spiker said as a shrill bell started to ring. 'See you in June!'

* * *

'It's so hot,' Grace said as she flung open the back door of her cottage one morning.

'Yes, I found it hard to sleep,' Rosie admitted as she pottered about the tiny kitchen in her robe.

'Let's have breakfast in the garden,' Grace suggested. 'I'll take the teapot out.'

'We can imagine we're back in Italy,' Rosie said. 'It must have been amazing for you, growing up there.'

'It was,' Grace said, 'but I'm so settled in England now, this feels like home, too.'

'What will you do when . . . '

'When I get married?' Grace asked.

'We want to live in England for at least a few years and see how it goes. Maybe we'll move back to Italy if and when the children arrive, but for the first years of marriage we're going to live here.'

'Ah,' Rosie said, 'so after you're married in August, I need to look for somewhere else. Unless of course I want to wear that green hairy suit permanently!'

' 'Fraid so,' Grace replied. 'But who knows? You could be married yourself by then.'

'Steady on.' Rosie crunched into her toast. 'I have to meet someone before I can get married.'

'But I thought . . . ' Grace raised one eyebrow. 'I thought after what I told you, what Roberto said, maybe David . . . You must think differently about him now? There's no obstacle in your way, is there? You should talk to him.'

'It's not that simple.' Rosie pulled the cord of her robe tighter around her waist. 'I know it's good news in a way that Donna wasn't perfect, in fact was obviously a very difficult person to be married to, but I think nevertheless David is still madly in love with her and doesn't want to be serious with anyone else.

'It's the only rational explanation of why he was so cold towards me after his organ recital back in the winter. We were getting on so well that day and then all of a sudden, out of nowhere, the shutters came down again. He isn't ready to fall in love again. He might never be.'

'And he hasn't tried to contact you again outside school, in all this time?' Grace asked.

'No. He's been perfectly civil at work but nothing romantic, not like before.'

'So there has been some romance between you,' Grace said eagerly. 'Spill the beans.'

'It's private,' Rosie said with a grin, 'but let's just say mistletoe was involved.'

Grace shrieked so loudly at that point that her neighbour next door, who was also enjoying a cup of tea in her garden, called out.

'Are you all right, Grace?'

'Perfectly fine, thank you,' Grace called back, choking with laughter.

'My goodness! Look at the time,' Rosie said as she sped inside to get dressed. 'We don't want to be late for work.'

Grace quickly finished her tea then followed Rosie into the cottage. She thought she might have to do spot of matchmaking to get David and Rosie sorted out.

She felt as certain now the two were a perfect match for each other as she had felt certain before David was not the right man for Rosie. You can't be too rational in affairs of the heart, she thought, as she bounded up the steep stairs to her bedroom to get dressed.

Too Close for Comfort

'I've found a special piano piece I want you to play at my farewell party,' Miss Spiker said to Rosie. 'It's a duet. I thought you could play it with Mr Hart. You'll need to practise it with him before the concert, I mean the party.'

'Thank you,' Rosie said as she took the ancient copy of 'Spanish Dances' held together with sticking plasters. 'Which dance would you like us to play?'

'Number Three,' Miss Spiker said. 'It has to be that one.'

Oh no, Rosie thought as she looked at the music. Why has she chosen that piece? I suppose it must be her favourite, but it's ridiculous to think David would want to play that with me, or I would want to play it with him. It's not proper, not for our situation.

'Mr Hart is waiting in the music

room for you now,' Miss Spiker continued. 'Chop chop — you know he doesn't like to be kept waiting.'

Rosie took her time going to join David. She visited the staff cloakroom first, to tidy herself up.

This is only to give me confidence, she reasoned with herself as she brushed her hair thoroughly to make it shine and applied quite a lot of red lipstick. I don't care at all what David thinks I look like, this is for me.

Spritzing herself with 'Charlie', a wise investment from the perfumery at Heathrow airport on the way out to Rome, Rosie set off to face David. Halfway to the music hut she realised she had left the copy of the 'Spanish Dances' next to the washbasin in the cloakroom and had to fly back into the main building to get the music.

'Looking for this?' Sister Anthony held the slightly soggy copy out to Rosie as she bumped into her in the corridor. 'Have a good rehearsal with Mr Hart, won't you? I believe you are playing an interesting piece together.'

How is it the nuns know everything that is going on, Rosie thought crossly.

By the time she finally got to the music hut she was out of breath and felt dishevelled.

'Hello,' David said, practising some menacing chords at the lower end of the piano. 'I gather we've been press-ganged into playing a duet for Miss Spiker at her party. Shall we get on with it? Should only take a quick once through.'

As David lifted his head and gazed at Rosie, he thought she had never looked so beautiful. She smelled divine, too.

'It's this one,' Rosie said, pointing at Dance Number Three.

'We can't play that!' David said in a shocked voice. 'It isn't at all suitable, for us I mean.'

'I know, but we have to,' Rosie said. 'Miss Spiker was very specific and it is for her special day.'

'Let's get it over with then,' David said. 'This speed should be about right

— one, two, three . . . '

'Hang on,' Rosie said. 'I wasn't ready. I've hardly even sat down yet!'

'Sorry. Try again. One, two, three . . . '

By the fourth bar of the piece, David had lifted his right arm over Rosie's left arm so that his right arm was playing in between her two hands, his shoulder unavoidably pushing against her shoulder and his body leaning towards hers.

Miss Spiker had chosen, on purpose, a piano duet involving crossing hands. She had decided that two of her favourite people needed a little help to get together and what better catalyst for this than music?

Rosie and David hurtled through the piece as one, getting faster and faster, with the vibrant Spanish rhythms crackling away until it sounded as if their fingers were on fire.

It might have been the glorious sunny weather or it might have been the excitement of the music and the crossing of the hands and the touching of the shoulders, but by the end of the piece Rosie and David felt a lot happier and more relaxed than at the beginning, so relaxed in fact that David forgot Rosie was supposedly going out with Tristan and Rosie forgot David wasn't interested in her because he was still in love with his deceased wife.

They moved even closer to each other, but before there could be a rerun of the mistletoe scene, David suddenly leaped away.

'I'm so sorry,' he said, 'I know you don't want this.'

'No, I'm sorry,' Rosie said. As she backed away from the piano, she felt more perplexed than ever.

Miss Spiker was disappointed to see Rosie again in the main building so quickly. She surmised correctly her masterplan hadn't worked and went as quickly as she could to inform Reverend Mother.

'Give it time,' Reverend Mother urged Miss Spiker. 'We mustn't give up.'

Special Day

A few weeks later, in early June, the day of Miss Spiker's party dawned without a cloud in the sky. Arabella had been training a choir of junior girls to sing a special tribute to Miss Spiker and she ran through all the dormitories early that morning to rouse the girls for an extra rehearsal.

'Come on, you lot,' she shouted as she banged on metal bedposts with a spoon borrowed from the refectory. 'Shake a leg! Time to get up. This is our last rehearsal and none of you are getting any breakfast before we've had a good run through.'

Lucy ran behind her, chivvying the girls and urging them to hurry. She had written the music for the choir to sing and was very excited to think of her composition having its first performance.

'This is going to be a world premiere,' she said to one girl who was showing reluctance to leave the comfort of her bed. 'You don't want to miss out, do you? The day girls have come in extra early so the least you can do is get out of bed.'

Once the girls had been lined up outside in the quad, Sophia organised them into a semi-circle.

'Sing your warm-up,' Arabella commanded, holding her hands up high to start them off.

'Stop talking,' Sophia said to the girls. 'You're meant to be singing.'

'This isn't as easy as it looks, is it?' Lucy said anxiously.

'It's fine,' Arabella said. 'They sound a bit tired, that's all. Now for the song . . . Ah, lovely. Well done. Everyone can go to breakfast now. Day girls, Sister Francis says you are invited to have breakfast with the boarders today.'

'Yippee!' Clementine shouted as she raced off after the others. 'Will there be toast?'

After delivering Clementine to school, Isobel had been standing watching the open air choir rehearsal. She was hoping to have a quick word with Arabella and seized her chance just before she joined the stampede to the refectory with the others.

'Thank you so much, Arabella, I can't tell you how grateful I am to you for reporting what you knew to the nuns and how you spoke to Clementine when she was being bullied. It means a lot to our family, to know there is a head girl like you who the younger girls can rely on. We are for ever in your debt.'

For once Arabella was lost for words.

As Isobel walked back to the car park, she saw Rosie arriving with Grace.

'Why, hello, Grace, how lovely to see you. It's been far too long,' Isobel said. 'And hello, Miss Peach.'

'Please do call me Rosie.'

'I'll try to remember.' Isobel looked at Rosie and thought what a great sister-in-law she would be. 'You look really well, Rosie. That's quite a tan you've got already this summer.'

'I've not had much time for sunbathing yet this term because we've been so busy in the music department,' Rosie said. 'The tan is left over from my Easter holiday. Grace here was kind enough to invite me out to Rome to stay with her family.'

'How fabulous,' Isobel said. 'I adore Italy. See you both later.'

That's interesting, Isobel thought as she walked back to her car. Rosie went abroad with Grace, not her new boyfriend as David had feared. I must remember to pass that on to David this afternoon.

* * *

There was a run though of all the music for the party during the morning and girls were summoned from various lessons at all sorts of times, making it more or less impossible for any proper teaching to be done.

By two p.m., cars had begun to sweep up the drive carrying parents who lived near enough to attend, old girls and staff, and Miss Spiker's special guests.

'Look!' Arabella cried from her vantage point at a window over the front door.

'There's that famous old girl. You know — the one who became a film star.'

'And there's the adjudicator from the festival in Bath,' Sophia shouted. 'He's so handsome!'

'Miss Spiker's arrived in a taxi,' Lucy pointed out. 'Arabella, aren't you supposed to . . . '

'Yes,' Arabella shrieked. 'I'm meant to be down there to greet her.'

Arabella made it downstairs in the nick of time to welcome Miss Spiker and show her to her seat in the hall.

'We're having the music first,' Arabella explained, 'then tea.'

'Can't wait,' Miss Spiker said. She sat

in the front row with a rapturous smile on her face, wearing a bright pink ruffled dress and white sandals, her hair artfully arranged in bubbly curls. 'What a thrill!'

The junior choir conducted by Arabella opened the show, with rapturous applause from the audience and a special bow taken by the composer, Lucy. Clementine played a short jazzy piano piece and Isobel squeezed Rod's fingers tightly as their daughter took a bow at the end.

David and Rosie's duet met with rapturous applause, but Tristan found it all rather baffling.

'I must say, they don't seem awfully fond of each other,' he muttered under his breath. 'In fact, they seem to be going to great lengths to avoid touching each other, which is very difficult in that particular duet.'

The next item was the senior choir performance.

Even better than in the autumn, Tristan thought. David knows his stuff and Rosie's always been a fine pianist.

When the girls had filed off the stage following their dazzling performance, Miss Spiker leaped to her feet.

'And now I'd like to invite Tristan Proudfoot to play something for us,' she announced.

'Thank you, thank you,' Tristan said. 'This is an arrangement of a special tune to say, 'Congratulations on your retirement' to Miss Dorcas Spiker.'

He strode to the piano and started improvising on 'Congratulations', much to the audience's delight. His hands flew up and down the keyboard, picking out the familiar notes of the melody and embellishing them in so many different and thrilling ways. The girls went wild at the end and Sophia dashed forward to present Tristan with a red rose.

'The only place to get a rose like that is from my rose garden,' Reverend Mother said, scowling.

'But it is a special day,' Sister Anne said.

'And Sophia only did it because she loves music,' Sister Anthony added.

And Tristan is a very handsome young man, Sister Francis reflected.

The concert came to a dignified end with Miss Spiker's performance of the 'Moonlight Sonata', then the entire audience made their way outside to the lower lawn where a splendid tea had been laid out on huge trestle tables.

'It's like a Royal garden party,' Rosie said in awe.

'And Miss Spiker's the Queen,' Grace added.

'I'm going to say hello to Tristan,' Rosie said. 'I didn't realise he knew Miss Spiker.'

Tristan was on the far side of the lower lawn, holding a large plate with three chocolate éclairs and four iced buns.

'Rosie,' he said, 'please don't look at me like that. I'll have you know I missed lunch.'

'I'm not judging you,' Rosie said. 'Actually I wanted to thank you, for that time you rescued me in Bath back in December and drove me home.'

'Glad to be of service,' Tristan replied. 'And about all that nonsense, Rosie, I behaved very badly, selfishly, but no matter because it's all sorted I gather. I expect your mother told you I rang while you were away in Rome with David? I'm very pleased for you both.'

'What are you talking about, Tristan? I didn't go to Rome with David and my mother didn't say you rang either. I have no idea what you mean.'

'Strange,' Tristan said. 'I must have misunderstood. Still, it explains the duet I suppose. Oh look, there's the man himself, over there. I'd better go and have a word.'

Before Rosie could stop Tristan, he was marching over to where David was chatting with his sister Isobel.

'You mean Rosie went to Rome with Grace at Easter? Not with Tristan?' David said to Isobel. 'This is good news, but it still doesn't mean . . . '

'I say, David,' Tristan said, interrupting David and Isobel, 'you and I need to talk. In private.'

A bewildered David allowed himself to be led by Tristan to the nuns' lawn, in front of the blue common room.

'Now look here,' Tristan began, 'what's going on? Are you going out with Rosie or not? You can't abandon a lovely girl like Rosie. I've a good mind to squish one of these éclairs into your face.'

'Of course I'm not going out with her,' David said. 'She's your girlfriend, isn't she? That's what you told me the last time I saw you.'

'Ah, about that . . . ' Tristan began hesitantly. 'Please don't think too badly of me, but . . . '

* * *

'Reverend Mother!' Arabella panted as she ran across the grass. 'Reverend Mother! There's a fight on the nuns' lawn. With cakes. And men. You have to come and stop them.'

'A fight?' Reverend Mother echoed. 'Cakes? Men? Sounds most unlikely. Lead me to it immediately.'

Lifting up her skirts, Reverend Mother ran after Arabella and found to her astonishment Tristan and David laughing heartily and slapping each other on the back like the very best of friends.

'Did you see a fight?' Reverend Mother whispered to Arabella.

'Not exactly,' Arabella replied, 'but they looked very angry and I thought they might fight.'

'They seem to have had some sort of altercation,' Reverend Mother said as she noticed some icing squished into Tristan's shirt and the remains of a chocolate éclair decorating David's shoulder, 'but all seems to be well now and I think we'll leave them to it, though I am cross they are on our lawn. That's strictly reserved for the nuns.'

Within a few minutes, all the girls in the school knew about the food fight and came flocking to see Tristan and David returning to the lower lawn and to civilised company.

'So you thought I was going out with Rosie all this time,' Tristan said incredulously to David.

'Because you told me you were going out with Rosie but not only was that not true, in fact she has never been out with you.' David's face was ecstatic and he looked as handsome as was possible for a man with sprinklings of choux pastry and cream stuck to the side of one of his ears.

'Do I hear the sound of obstacles falling away?' Isobel asked.

'I think I understand now what's been going on,' Rosie said. 'It makes sense at last.'

'It's more complicated than an opera plot,' Tristan chipped in.

David and Rosie smiled at each other and held hands, daring to hope they had a bright future together.

'Joy,' Miss Spiker said, the ruffles on her pink dress fluttering as she clapped her hands and attempted to jump up and down.

'Perfect,' the nuns chorused in unison.

'About time,' Grace added.

Epilogue:
July 1976

'I can't believe it's over three weeks since Miss Spiker's retirement party,' Rosie whispered to herself as she lay under the shade of the beech tree high up on the hilltop, the shimmering sky above painted a cloudless Wedgwood blue.

Picking up her book again, she read a few more pages.

'I hope I have more luck in love than you, Tess Durbeyfield.'

Gently encouraging a ladybird to move off the page, Rosie was startled to hear a voice behind her.

'You will if I have anything to do with it.'

'David!' she cried and sprang to her feet to greet him. 'I thought we weren't meeting up this afternoon? You said you had to go to Salisbury and would ring me later.'

'My shopping trip didn't take as long as I thought it would,' David said.

'Hang on . . . your shopping trip? And how did you know I'd be here?'

'I rang Grace's cottage and when there was no reply I rang the convent for information and spoke to Sister Anne. Apparently you told her yesterday you were planning to relax up here under a tree with a book and she thought it was an excellent way to spend Saturday afternoon.'

'How clever you are,' Rosie murmured, holding her arms out to David.

'We'll have none of that, young lady, not until I've made my speech anyway and you've seen the result of my trip to Salisbury.'

'Your speech? Your trip? What . . . '

David dropped to one knee and pulled a small box out of his pocket.

'It matches your eyes,' he said as he opened the box to show an exquisite emerald ring. 'Rosie, would you do me the great honour . . . '

'Of course,' she squealed and pulled him to his feet. 'Of course I'll marry you. I love you, David Hart.'

'And I love you, Rosie Peach,' David murmured as he took her in his arms and kissed her thoroughly. 'I've loved you ever since I first saw you hurrying down the drive for your interview last autumn, with that ridiculous horse chestnut case stuck in your hair.'

After a while they both looked out from the hilltop over the hazy parched fields.

'We have a problem, though . . . ' Rosie began.

'No more obstacles,' David said with a groan. 'Surely we've overcome everything possible! What is it this time?'

Rosie grinned.

'It's just that I happen to know three hundred girls who will all want to be my bridesmaids!'

Other titles in the Linford Romance Library:

MELTING EVIE'S HEART

Jill Barry

Film-set director Evie is between projects, and hurting from being dumped by the arrogant Marcus. Escaping to spend Christmas in her parents' idyllic countryside home, what will finally lift her mood — her mum's relentless festive spirit, the cosiness of village traditions . . . or the attention of gorgeous antiques dealer Jake? When the leading duo in this year's village pantomime drops out after a bust-up, Evie and Jake are roped in to take over. But with Evie playing the princess, just how seriously will Jake take his new role as Prince Charming?